Love and Modern Medicine

BOOKS BY PERRI KLASS

FICTION

Recombinations

I Am Having an Adventure: Stories

Other Women's Children

Love and Modern Medicine

NONFICTION

A Not Entirely Benign Procedure:
Four Years as a Medical Student

Baby Doctor: A Pediatrician's Training

Love and Modern Medicine

STORIES

PERRI KLASS

A MARINER ORIGINAL
Houghton Mifflin Company
Boston · New York
2001

Visit our Web site: www.houghtonmifflinbooks.com.

Library of Congress Cataloging-in-Publication Data
Klass, Perri, date.
Love and modern medicine : stories / Perri Klass.
p. cm.
"A Mariner original."
ISBN 0-618-10960-9
1. United States—Social life and customs—20th century—
Fiction. 2. Women physicians—fiction. 3. Women scientists—
Fiction. 4. Mother and child—Fiction. 5. Domestic
fiction, American. I. Title.
PS3561.L248 L68 2001
813'.54—dc21 00-066978

Printed in the United States of America

Book design by Robert Overholtzer

QUM 10 9 8 7 6 5 4 3 2 1

The following stories have also appeared, sometimes in slightly
different form, in these publications: "For Women Everywhere" and
"Intimacy" in *Glamour;* "Rainbow Mama" in *North American
Review;* "Necessary Risks," "City Sidewalks," "Freedom Fighter,"
"Dedication," and "The Trouble with Sophie" in *Redbook;*
"Exact Change" in *Story;* and "The Province of the
Bearded Fathers" in *Missouri Revew.*

In memory of William Abrahams,
with love

Contents

Love and Modern Medicine

For Women Everywhere

ALISON, in her ninth month, finds she can no longer turn over in bed at night without waking up. The hydraulics of shifting her belly are just too complex, and to get from her left side to her right, she has to maneuver herself delicately, tucking her elbow under and using it as a lever, swinging her abdomen over the top. Turning over the other way, belly down, is not possible; if she could, she imagines, she would look like a circus seal balancing on a huge ball.

When her best friend from high school arrives to keep her company and wait for the birth, Alison hopes to be distracted; lately, she thinks of nothing but the advent of labor. When will this baby come out, when will the pains start that will be unmistakably something new, something she has never felt before? Her obstetrician suggested that they might feel like bad menstrual cramps, which Alison has never had. And she is now accustomed to the small tightenings inside her belly that occur every now and then; Braxton-Hicks contraction, she tells her friend Doris, who thereafter asks her, if she should happen to clutch herself, "Another Brixie-Hixie?"

It is very nice to have Doris around. For one thing, unpregnant, Doris is easily as big as Alison in her ninth month. Doris was big in high school and she's bigger now. She buys her clothes in special stores that sell silk and velvet and linen for the fat working woman, and all her lingerie is peach. She smells of a perfume named after a designer, familiar to Alison because of little scented cardboard samples in a million magazines – open this flap to enjoy the magic – opposite honey-toned photos of naked bodies arranged like fruit in a basket. Doris's possessions fit surprisingly well into what she calls the tawdry jungle glamour of Alison's apartment. Among the overgrown plants with Christmas lights strung through them and the life-size stuffed animals and the bongo collection, Doris reclines in her jumpsuits, taking her ease as if waiting for her palanquin. When Doris and Alison walk down the street together on their way to get hamburgers and onion rings, Alison feels like they are a phalanx. Finally she has the nerve to wear a big straw hat with fuchsia flowers out in public, stealing it off her stuffed giraffe. Hey, big mamas, she imagines someone shouting (not that anyone ever does). Together, she and Doris take up their share of the street and of the hamburger restaurant, where the waitress greets them by saying, The usual, right?

Alison is by now pretty well used to the rude and stupid and none-of-their-business things that people say to her. But good old Doris walked into her apartment, put down her two suitcases and her handbag and her camera case, and informed Alison, looking narrowly at her ballooned abdomen, "Alison, you are doing this For Women Everywhere." Then she gave a Bronx cheer.

"Right," said Alison with relief, wondering how Doris knew. The world is full of well-meaning people who feel the need to tell Alison how brave she is, how they admire her. I always wanted a baby, but I don't know whether I would dare, they say; or, This is a really great thing you're doing. Alison's mother sends clippings from *People* magazine, keeping her up to date on Jodie Foster, Madonna, Rosie O'Donnell. Even Michael, when he calls up, shyly, to ask does she really think this baby might be his, and won't she please tell him when it's due, and is she going to find out the gender, and would she tell him if she knew — even Michael feels a politically correct need to tell her what a strong woman she is.

"Some people never grow up" is Doris's comment after Michael's next call. At first Alison thinks she is referring to Michael, which is really unfair; of the three of them, Michael could be considered the one who most notably *has* grown up. He has a house and a marriage and two children and all the correct car seats and coffeemakers. "You," says Doris. "Here you are at your age, and the best you can manage is a friend you went to high school with and a boy you've been sleeping with since high school. Don't you ever think about moving on to a later stage?"

There is some justice there, Alison supposes, but if you are thirty-five and your favorite people are left over from when you were fifteen, then that's the way it is. *What am I doing, after all,* she thinks, *if not moving on to a later stage?* Michael's marriage, acquired in adulthood, does not make Alison's mouth water. Neither does Doris's legendary liaison with a penthouse-dwelling real estate tycoon. Doris is mildly, or maybe avidly, curious to know who the other possible fathers are, and makes some pointed remarks about people who expect their friends to Tell All and then hold back on their own juicy details, but Alison is not telling and not willing to be drawn into the same game of twenty questions that Michael keeps wanting her to play. Is it anyone I know? Is it anyone you care about? How many possibilities are there, anyway? "I am not," Alison says with pregnant dignity, "the kind to kiss and tell."

Alison is consuming something close to four rolls of Tums a day at this point. Automatically before and after every meal she reaches into her pocket for the cylinder, pops off three little chalky disks, and crunches them, feeling the burning go away.

Doris tells her this is somewhat disgusting, and Alison informs her loftily, "My obstetrician says I have progesterone-induced incompetence of the lower esophageal sphincter."

"Talk about disgusting," says Doris.

But it is a pleasure to have Doris there to go with her to the obstetrician, a pleasure not to go alone for the umpteenth time. She hands Doris the straw hat and steps on the scales unhesitatingly, watches the nurse move the weight from 150 to 200, then back to 150, then start messing around with the next smaller weight. One eighty-two; very good. Smugly, Alison steps off the scale; how educational for Doris, she thinks, to realize that when you are pregnant you get on the scale proudly and hear a number like 182 and then a commendation. But Doris is studying a wall chart, a drawing of a full-term baby packed into a mother. Note the scrunched-up intestines, the way the baby's head presses on the bladder, and so on. "Yich," comments Doris, and follows Alison into the examining room, there to be notably unmoved by the amplified fetal heart.

Alison's obstetrician, Dr. Beane, is a good five or six years younger than Alison and Doris, and is such an immaculate and tailored little thing that it is hard to imagine her elbow-deep in the blood and gore that Alison envisions in a delivery room. Also, she has such tiny hands; can she really grab a baby and pull? Is that what an obstetrician does? Alison started by dutifully attending the classes, but she dropped out long before they got to the movie; she has never been one to read instruction booklets. Dr. Beane gives Doris the once-over, considerately doesn't ask any questions, and feels around on Alison's belly with those small, surprisingly strong hands. "You're engaged!" she says, as if offering congratulations.

Alison wonders briefly whether this is some terribly tactful way of acknowledging Doris's presence (better than, say, Is this your significant other?), but it turns out that *engaged* means the baby's head has descended into her pelvis and the baby is in place, ready to be born.

"Have you thought about anesthesia?" asks the doctor, who then launches into an educational lecture on spinals and epidurals, both of which involve having a needle inserted into Alison's back and pumping drugs into her spinal column.

"Yich," comments Doris.

"I think I'd rather die," says Alison.

"You won't die one way or the other. You'll just have pain. And if the pain is too bad, you can have Demerol, just to take the edge off for a while."

"In sorrow shall you bring forth children," says Doris, biblically enough.

"Pay no attention to that man behind the curtain," says Alison, not to be outdone.

"Any time now," says Dr. Beane, cheerful and unperturbed.

Twenty years ago, in high school, Doris and Alison and Michael were the three smartest of their year, Doris and Alison were best friends, and Michael and Alison eventually fumbled their way into bed. Michael and Doris, however, were the true co-conspirators of the high school, the ones who destroyed every sewing machine in the home economics classroom with a tube of Super Glue and a jar of Vaseline, the ones who reprogrammed the guidance computer so that every senior received a printout recommending Notre Dame as the most appropriate college, the ones who slipped copies of *Oui* and *Penthouse* into the heavy plastic jackets reserved for *Life* and *Smithsonian* in the library. Alison was more or less a chicken. Doris is now the only person in the whole world who more or less understands how Alison can go on sleeping with Michael every couple of weeks or so, year in and year out, and never want either to escalate or to de-escalate. There are other guys around from time to time, but in a funny way she still likes Michael best — even though she doesn't like him more than once every couple of weeks. And when Michael got married and they didn't miss a beat, Doris was the only one to whom it was perfectly obvious that his relationship with Alison was covered by a grandfather clause. Alison knows that Michael called Doris up at the time, stricken with the kind of moral qualms with which he occasionally likes to agitate himself, and she knows that Doris told him to shut up and put out, and she is grateful. Michael's marriage is a brilliant success, as far as Alison can see, though she has not actually met his wife. They are both professors, Michael of math, of course, and his wife of something with ceramics in it, which is not art but high-tech semiconductors. Or something; Alison reserves the right not to be interested and wastes almost no time visualizing the marriage, two total weirdo science drones trying to be domestic. She has never imagined that this is what she wants, and she is not going to be fooled into imagining it now.

Alison and Doris parade themselves to the hamburger joint for the usual once again. Alison has medium rare with cheddar and onions, Doris has rare with guacamole on top; both have onion rings. Alison's maternity wardrobe has dwindled; nothing fits, and she cannot bring herself to buy anything, since the whole process should be over in a week or two. She has one floral drop cloth, contributed by her mother, who also sent four pairs of support hose that are still intact in their plastic.Over her one pair of cotton pants with a very stretched-out elastic waistband she can put either a bright pink, extra-extra large T-shirt or a breezy little yellow rayon number, bought at a yard sale, which was meant to be a pajama top for a very large lady. She has been working at home since her seventh month, easy enough since much of her work has always been done at home. She writes the in-house newsletter for a large company that manufactures communications equipment and works happily on various examples of their latest technology right in the comfort of her own living room. She is paid a ridiculous amount for this and has no intention of ever teaching freshman English again. The only problem, as of the last week or two, is that she cannot sit up at her desk anymore for long periods of time. The inhabitant of her uterus starts to do calisthenics, and to have a full-size baby doing rhythmic jerks in her belly, it turns out, means she has to lie back on the couch and give it room.

She lies back, pulls up the pink T-shirt, pulls down the cotton pants, and she and Doris stare at her stomach, at the road map of stretch marks. "God, it's like some kind of earthquake," says Doris, as the striated skin over Alison's belly button heaves upward. Today Doris, in honor of Alison's apartment, is wearing her leopard-print jumpsuit and blood-red earrings to match her fingernails.

"Are you quite comfortable?" Alison asks her abdomen. The acute angle of a little elbow juts out clearly, squirms around, then retreats into its crowded bath. Actually, Alison finds herself overwhelmed, reduced to awestruck mush, by the contemplation of her belly, by the thought that tightly curled up in there is a full-grown sardine of a baby. How can this possibly be? A fetus was one thing, for all its hormonal cyclone, the morning sickness and all the rest, but how can she be carrying around something that properly belongs in a baby carriage? And something with such a mind of its own; it seems now to want to put its feet just where Alison believes she keeps her liver.

When Michael calls, Doris takes it upon herself to talk to him. She describes the action in Alison's belly, which she refers to as heavy weather in the Himalayan foothills. Alison, still lying on the couch, can hear the firm tones in which Doris discourages Michael's surreptitious questions. She's fine, we're fine, don't be ridiculous. Sometime soon, you don't need the details. No, Michael, you'll never know. You'll take care of your own children, Alison will take care of hers, and everyone will be just fine.

Alison thinks of Doris in the tenth grade, when she wore only black and made frequent references to her dabbles in the occult sciences. Her room, in her parents' pleasant Tudor-style, two-car-garage house, had been converted into a sanctuary of Satan. Doris had removed the light bulb from the ceiling fixture and put two white, skull-shaped candles on either side of an altar, on which the girls' high school gym teacher was regularly tortured in effigy before being sacrificed. Doris's mother had minded the writing on the walls more than anything else. But after all, once the walls were written on they would have to be repainted anyway, so why not write on them some more? So Doris and Alison and Michael decorated them freely with song lyrics that seemed particularly meaningful at the time. Also poems. The Who, William Blake, Hermann Hesse, and Leonard Cohen figured prominently in the graffiti; Doris and Alison and Michael were all smart, but hardly exceptional. Anyway, lying on the couch, Alison remembers Doris in her high priestess phase: massive in black, making oracular pronouncements, suggesting death or disfigurement for those she disliked, promising the favored that they would prosper.

"Lots of Brixie-Hixies, huh?" says Doris a few minutes later, finding Alison leaning against the wall in the kitchen, holding her stomach.

"I don't know, this might be more than that."

"No false alarms now – you don't want to go getting me all excited for nothing."

"Let's time them," says Alison.

Twenty minutes apart. Fifteen minutes apart. Starting to hurt a little. Lasting thirty to forty seconds. Doris notes them down systematically in permanent Magic Marker on Alison's one clean dish towel, contributed, needless to say, by her mother.

She suggests to Alison that these numbers will make a humdrum dish towel into a priceless memento. Alison tries to remember whether they said anything about breathing back in those first couple of childbirth classes.

"All right," says Doris, coming to the bottom hem of the dish towel. "Get that cunning little bag you have all packed and waiting and let's get moving."

"You really think it's time?"

"Do you want to wait for Sherman to take Atlanta? Get into the pony cart and let's go."

At the hospital, the nurse puts Alison into two little gowns, one with the opening in the front, the other in the back. Strangely enough, all the way over in the car, even as she experimented with panting, with taking big deep breaths, with moaning and groaning, Alison expected the hospital staff to look at her blankly, to send her home, to wonder aloud why she was wasting their time. Instead, along comes this nurse, Madeline, a black woman even larger than Doris. *The three of us,* Alison thinks, *would make quite a singing group.* The nurse puts an IV into Alison's left hand and hooks belts around her waist to connect her to a fetal heart monitor. Doris finds the monitor quite interesting, and when the nurse leaves the room, she experiments with the volume control, turning up the gallop-a-trot of the baby's heartbeat as loud as it will go.

"Noisy baby you have there," she remarks. "I thought this was supposed to hurt. Does it hurt yet?"

"Are you looking forward to watching me writhe in pain?"

"Just remember, you will be writhing for women everywhere."

Alison is immeasurably glad to have Doris there. Does this mean, she finds two seconds to wonder in between contractions, that she is in fact going to want someone there from now on, that she is going to find herself alone with this baby and feel bereft? Well, maybe. But this is a fine time to start worrying about that.

"Don't worry," she tells Doris. "It's starting to hurt plenty. Don't be deceived by my stoicism and physical bravery." A baby is supposed to make you less alone, not more alone, she reminds herself, and then the pain is back.

"When you make a face like you're constipated and then pant like a dog, is that when it hurts?"

"I still can't understand why you didn't become a psychiatrist," says Alison, beginning to pant again.

"There's more money in stockbrokering," says Doris, who is in fact very rich.

"Well, thanks for coming," says Alison, suddenly not sure she has yet gotten around to saying that.

"I wouldn't miss this for the world." Doris looms over the bed, a great big woman with an auburn permanent and red nails, wearing green paisley lounging pajamas. What more could anyone want in a labor room? "Soon the fun will really begin — don't you get an enema?"

"I think that's out of date. Shit, Doris, this isn't a joke anymore."

"All you girls think you can just play around, and then when you get caught, you start whining."

Madeline comes bustling in, hears them shouting over the boom of the monitor. "Who turned this thing up so high?" she demands, turning it down.

"I want to take this belt off, please," says Alison. "I feel like I need to change position."

"Why don't you take a little walk, see some of the scenery?" Madeline is unstrapping her from the monitor, rather to Alison's surprise; she hadn't expected her request to be granted.

"Is that okay?"

"Honey, you're moving pretty quick for a first baby, but

you've got a ways to go. Just you go strolling with your friend, there's lots of corridors."

The people that Alison and Doris pass as they promenade through the Labor and Delivery hallways look meaningfully at Alison's belly. Most are doctors and nurses dressed in green surgical scrubs. There is one other woman in labor who is also up and walking, but her husband, who is six feet tall and bearded after the manner of John the Baptist, is practically carrying her. The walls are hung with nondescript impressionist landscapes.

"Lovely on the Riviera this time of year," Doris says each time they pass the French fishing village, and "I hear the stained glass is simply stunning," when they pass the cathedral at sunset.

Eventually walking begins to feel a little less possible, and Alison climbs back into bed. And along comes Dr. Beane to congratulate her on already being five centimeters dilated.

"God," says Alison, "this is becoming a real pain in the ass."

"Truer words were never spoken," says Doris.

Alison is no longer able to muster a sense of humor. She is in quite significant pain, and it is borne in upon her that she does not have the option of stopping these regular onslaughts. She would like an hour off, she wants to tell them; she would like to put this on hold and start again tomorrow. Instead, Madeline comes by every now and then and tells her to take deep breaths. They have her belted up again and keep telling her to listen to her baby's heart, how strong and regular it is. But this steady lub-a-dubbing seems to Alison to have very little indeed to do with the strong-willed gymnast who has been kicking and wriggling so idiosyncratically. Alison wishes, truly and sincerely, to be back on her couch, watching her stomach heave and swell. What a good working relationship that was — why go and spoil it now?

"I didn't know when I was well off," she tells Doris and Madeline. Dr. Beane is somewhere behind them, checking the strips that the monitor is printing out. An interesting geometrical dynamic, thinks Alison with perfect clarity, the three very large women and the tiny little doctor.

In fact, it goes very quickly for a first labor; everyone says so. Five hours after coming to the hospital, Alison is pronounced ready to push. Alison is no longer listening to anything that anyone has to say. This is, she has decided, the most ridiculous method for propagating the species that she can imagine. In those few precious seconds when the pain goes away, she thinks back to biology class, herself and Doris and Michael in the back row, acing every test. Think of all the alternative methods. Budding. Spore formation. Egg laying. Binary fission. And back comes the pain; howling, she has discovered, helps. Madeline does not seem to approve fully; there was something a little censorious about the way she closed the labor room door. "Mustn't let the other women in labor know that it hurts, huh?" Alison hears Doris say.

Sometimes she squeezes Doris's hand. Sometimes Doris squeezes hers. During one particularly unpleasant contraction, Alison gives out with a loud cry of "Oh, fuckety fuck fuck the fucking fuck," and then her brain clears enough to hear Doris's response: "Do any more of that, darling, and you'll end up right back here."

What can she mean? Another contraction hits before Alison can actually think back to those familiar and surprisingly passionate nights with Michael, or to the nights with the other two men who will never know about this. Oddly enough, she can remember, as the pain ebbs, her decision to go ahead and get pregnant, that one particularly promising and active month when she got herself into this. *It's time to do this,* she remembers thinking, remembers that daring feeling of dancing on the cliff edge. *I will surprise myself, my life will stretch and grow,* she remembers thinking. And now she has fallen off the cliff. Something is stretching, sure enough, and surprise is not the word for it. Yes, she can remember deciding to get pregnant, but her brain cannot quite encompass the how of getting pregnant. Out of the question. This is no moment to think about the more pleasant uses to which her lower body can be put. This is a moment to howl.

Dr. Beane, who has been off doing doctor things, reappears after Alison has been pushing for half an hour or so. Pushing is a little better than just contracting, but it is also hard work. "I have had enough of this," Alison tells her, loud and clear. "There is never going to be a baby. I want to go home."

"You're doing very, very well. You're going to have your baby soon."

"I don't want a baby. I changed my mind." She is dead serious, she is enjoying being a bad girl, she is kidding, she is contracting again, and Madeline is counting at her, ten nine eight seven six five four three two one, trying to get Alison to prolong the push.

"You heard the lady. She's changed her mind." Doris almost sounds dead serious herself.

Dr. Beane puts Doris on one side of Alison, Madeline on the other. Alison puts one arm around each of them, and each lifts up one of her legs, pulls it back. Dr. Beane is now a tiny pixie all dressed in surgical greens, rubber gloves on her hands. She looks at Alison severely. "You need to push this baby out," she says. "The monitor is showing poor beat-to-beat variability, and you are ready to do it!"

"What is poor beat-to-beat variability?" asks Doris. Alison doesn't care.

"It means she has to push this baby out. Now, pull back on her legs. Madeline will count, and on the next push I want to see progress."

It takes exactly sixteen more pushes for the baby to be born.

Alison is complaining for the first several pushes; she has suddenly remembered that she was promised Demerol for pain and is demanding it loudly. Dr. Beane tells her, somewhat brusquely, that she cannot have it so close to delivery, and Alison begins to make a speech about how unfair this is, how she has labored and labored and pushed and pushed. Then two things happen at once: another contraction begins, and Doris leans in close to her ear and says loudly, "Stop whining and push! Something's going wrong with the baby!"

And, amazingly enough, Alison does care. Or at least responds. Or at least feels she has to respond. Or something. She stops making speeches, she grips the two pillars on either side and bears down for the full count. Dr. Beane encourages her. "I see the head!" she calls from her little steel stool between Alison's legs. Toward the end, Alison loses track of everything. She keeps her eyes fixed on Madeline's, since Madeline is the one who tells her, *This will be it, you'll do it next time.* She bears down when Madeline counts, responding to the authoritative numbers like Pavlov's dog. And then, at the end, everything changes. Instead of pure pain and effort and her body straining and close to exploding, she actually feels it, she does, she feels something move down, something fall away from her, something slide out of her, and the next moment everyone is laughing and cheering.

There is no separating anything out: Dr. Beane's triumphant announcement that she has a girl, the sudden shocking cries, slightly thin and then outraged, Madeline's assurances from across the room that the baby is perfect, ten fingers and ten toes. Before Alison can even contemplate that information, the baby, wrapped in a somewhat bloody blanket, is deposited on her chest. Only then, lying back, does Alison realize the pain has actually stopped.

Dr. Beane and Madeline are still messing around at the bottom of the bed. Alison and Doris, however, are busy admiring the baby, who has stopped crying and is scrunched up in her mother's arms, occasionally opening her eyes to see if she can see who is responsible for this outrage. A little stretchy white cap on her head works its way off, and it turns out she has a great deal of dark hair. To Alison's relief, she looks like a newborn, like a monkey; there is no uncanny resemblance to Michael or any other adult.

"She's certainly beautiful," Doris says, as if surprised. Actually, she isn't particularly beautiful, Alison supposes, but then, on the other hand, she's the most miraculously divinely beautiful thing ever.

"I know what you mean."

"What happens now?" Doris asks, after a lull of admiring, during which Dr. Beane finishes up with the afterbirth and the stitches; a few twinges and a few ouches from Alison, but she is harder to impress than she used to be. The baby, eyes closed, nuzzles into her mother's neck, seeking warmth, or food, or contact, maybe missing the close confinement where up to now she has rocked and kicked and wriggled.

"Now Mother goes on up to the maternity floor and gets a little rest," says Madeline, "and Baby goes to the nursery and gets weighed and measured."

"Now I guess I take her home and educate her," says Alison, in wonderment.

"Well, good," says Doris. "As long as you have a plan."

Rainbow Mama

As long as she lives, Peggy will never forgive herself for the fight she had with her mother only last week. Came up to visit and insisted on taking Peggy and Jerry out to Burger King, even though Peggy doesn't like for him to eat too much junk. And then, sitting uncomfortably in one of those plastic molded seats which nowhere near fit her curves, Peggy had to listen to her mother starting in on Jerry because he didn't finish his fries. He didn't eat anything, Peggy, he doesn't eat enough. I'm worried about him, he looks so thin, you ought to see to it that he finishes his food. And so right there in Burger King, she couldn't resist letting her mother have it. Lay off, she said. Remember, you nagged me and nagged me about finishing my food when I was a kid, and look at me now. And defiantly, her own food all eaten up, she finished Jerry's fries for him while he sucked idly on a shake.

His grandmother had also brought him a new box of crayons, and Peggy took out the pad she always carries; she and her mother sat on in mutually wounded silence while Jerry colored, then brought them back together by showing them: the airplane in the sky and soldiers shooting down the plane, but it's a good plane! Oh no, said Peggy, thinking she shouldn't let him watch the news, ever. But Jerry told her reassuringly, It's okay, because even though it's a good plane, the bad people are flying it.

If it had been a high fever, she would have taken Jerry to the pediatrician right away; she's always been careful. When she reads the magazines on the checkout line at the Stop and Shop, she always reads the articles about danger signs, household hazards. High fever, stiff neck, head injuries, she knows all about, and how a few adult aspirins can kill a toddler. She doesn't buy the magazines; she's not one for the arts and crafts. Why make a quilted Christmas wreath out of calico when you can buy one made of evergreens? And thirty different things to do with chopped meat leave her cold. Anyway, she's busy, she doesn't have much time, especially with her husband gone and her travel agency becoming so successful. Jerry likes drumsticks and corn on the cob, and so does she, baked potatoes and good-quality all-beef kosher franks. Nothing fancy, but not junk either.

The low fever has been coming and going for a week when she finally takes Jerry to the pediatrician, expecting, really, that he'll tell her it's nothing, it's a bug, Tylenol and lots of fluids and plenty of rest. So she's let it go on for a week, another thing she'll never forgive. The pediatrician feels things under Jerry's arms, lymph glands, and feels something in his belly, his spleen; the pediatrician suddenly looks very interested, too interested, his careful hands insinuating themselves one more time into Jerry's armpits.

Peggy doesn't call Noah from the emergency room that afternoon, something *he'll* probably never forgive, but that's not her problem. He's Jerry's father, okay, but he walked out on her, walked out on his kid. One weekend afternoon every now and then doesn't mean shit, and she doesn't want him in the cubicle where she waits while they are doing the bone marrow biopsy on Jerry. Doesn't want anyone else there at all, not the nurse who keeps looking in, concerned, to tell her one more time where the coffee machine is. Peggy stares at oxygen tubing coming out of the wall, green and glittering in the fluorescent light, her mother's kind of color. I'd like to have a dress to match, her mother will say, pointing to the most unlikely things: the yellow letters on the digital alarm clock, the purple foil around one of Jerry's fruit pops. Peggy might have been a nurse, might have belonged in a hospital, but she met Noah and got sidetracked, began wandering around to craft fairs with him and selling the jewelry he made. And then Jerry, four years ago, taking care of Jerry and settling down, and lately managing on her own. Now she could never be a nurse; think how they get ordered around. She finds herself wishing for her office, her computer in front of her, the phone with all the lines at her elbow, some confused client across the desk. Well, Peggy is explaining kindly, there are a lot of different kinds of cruises.

She can hear a child screaming down the corridor, but it doesn't sound like Jerry, and they promised her they would give him local anesthetic. In her hand, Peggy is clutching the picture Jerry made for her while they were waiting for a doctor to come see him. She was trying to act normal; he was cheerful and himself, with no idea what was in store. It is a picture of a monster, but a good monster, so there are two children riding on his back, but the evil knight is flying on a dragon to catch them, but one of the children is really Peter Pan, so he has a sword and he can fight the evil knight. There has to be some way to go back, here, now, while she is in this room, before anyone has come to bring her news. But go back how far? Before the fever started — she is remembering what happened in the Burger King. And the way the doctor in the emergency room said, "He looks a little bit thin — has he lost weight recently?" To her, Jerry looks delicate and beautiful, lent to her in his perfect grace. Surely there is some way to go back, to start when life was on track, and then rush it like a zipper over the broken part, holding things together.

No news is bad news. They tell her they can't give her any answers yet, they admit Jerry to the hospital, they tell her everyone will be around to discuss the situation a little later on. There are two beds in the hospital room, both empty. Jerry, who now looks to her so skinny and fragile he is liable to fragment like a pretzel stick, lies quietly on one of them, watching the television that comes down from the ceiling like an octopus's sucker. Tired out from crying, Peggy thinks, the blood tests, the bone marrow biopsy. But the questions nag at her — Any bruising you've noticed? There was that black-and-blue spot on his side from when he fell against the coffee table, and it hasn't gone away. And has he seemed tireder than usual lately? She hovers over Jerry, finally sits gingerly on the side of his bed, wondering if he will turn to her, ask her what is happening, why it's happening, What have I done? But when he turns to her, it is to grant her a smile that she does not feel she has deserved at all and to bargain with her anxiously: Can I watch for more than one hour tonight? Because it isn't our TV at home, so the rule is different, right? Can I watch as much as I want? And a little later she finally looks up from Jerry to the TV, sees that it is cops and shooting, the kind of show she never lets him watch, and her son looks at her with guilt and mischief in his eyes. It isn't really scary, he assures her, it won't give me bad dreams. It's just shooting and guns, and you know I like to see guns if they aren't real. Peggy hopes devoutly that he will dream only of guns; she wraps her arms around him and they watch the show together.

When the meeting finally happens, Peggy is upset by how crowded it is. There is Peggy, who has insisted that Noah cannot be reached, so there is only Peggy. There are three different doctors: Dr. Richardson, who is the oncologist, tall and thin and calm, and another oncologist who is younger, fatter, and more nervous, and then this funny-looking balding boy named Dale Dooley, who introduces himself by saying, I'm just the intern. And there are two nurses as well, and another woman, who turns out to be the oncology social worker.

After all of which, it could hardly be said to come as a surprise that Jerry has leukemia. Peggy is no dummy; she knew as she watched the cast assemble that they had not come to tell her, Sorry you were worried, false alarm, Tylenol, fluids, rest. Dr. Richardson does the talking. He makes a lot of eye contact, speaks slowly, and takes trouble to explain his words. Peggy understands that he has done this many times, this scene.

"First of all, Jerry does have leukemia. Now, let me explain to you exactly what leukemia is . . ." He explains to her as if he thinks she's dumb; she knows what blood cells are, what bone marrow is. She'll never suck on a marrow bone again, not after Jerry today. Now he's onto chemotherapy, telling her that the drugs have to be toxic to cells in order to kill the cancer, but you can't choose which cells, so there will be effects on other cells in the body that divide quickly. Nausea. Hair loss. He pauses at hair loss, and Peggy senses that she is supposed to say something. The oncology social worker puts in, "Many parents find the idea of hair loss one of the most upsetting things of all." The oncology social worker is a skinny lady with a big chest, expensively dressed in dark red angora, dress and matching sweater. It makes Peggy itch just to look at her.

Well, of course it's upsetting. Jerry has silky black hair, his father's hair but purer. But who the hell is going to worry about hair at this point?

"I want to know whether you think he's going to die," she says, and then sees from their faces that they have been expecting the question.

"I think his chances are excellent," Dr. Richardson is saying, promising more definite answers when they get back some special tests, telling her how much worse off Jerry would have been if he had gotten this disease twenty years ago. Twenty years ago I was ten years old, Peggy feels like saying. Fuck twenty years ago.

They are so concerned to answer her questions. They are so eager to explain. They are so proud of their drugs, the hope, the advantage of now over even ten years ago. The social worker tells her, "I know this is very stressful for you, and I want you to know that we're all here for you, that we plan to support you as well as Jerry; that's part of our job. You should feel free to ask for any kind of support you need, and I want you to feel free to share your feelings with me, whatever they may be."

"Thank you for your concern," Peggy says politely. They all wait. "Thank you so much for your support." They wait. "When it comes right down to it, though, you are a bunch of perfect strangers, and I am not about to let you see me cry." But she might have cried after all, right there and then, if she had not happened to catch Dale Dooley's eye. He looked at her admiringly, nodded his head emphatically.

Intravenous lines, and chemotherapy, and finally that evening she calls Noah and breaks it to him over the phone, flat and informative. Noah is living, when last heard from, with yet another woman, not the one he left Peggy for. Peggy wishes with all her heart that Noah could have cancer instead of Jerry; Noah is not much good to anyone, and is so fucking self-righteous these days about whole foods, he deserves a fatal disease. It is Peggy's job to inform and comfort Noah over the phone so he can calm down enough to drive to the hospital and break down all over again. He finds Peggy up in Jerry's bed, Jerry leaning against her thigh, watching something or other, the two of them beyond fatigue and upset. Noah has to go out and pick a fight with the soda machine, which gives him regular Coke instead of the no-caffeine Coke he wanted for Jerry.

Peggy does maybe the meanest thing she has ever done in her whole life on Friday, and she doesn't feel a bit bad about it either. It is day number five of Jerry's protocol, which is a big deal; he gets another bone marrow biopsy and a spinal tap, and they inject chemotherapy right into his spine through a hollow needle. It turns out she can come with him for all this; Dale Dooley told her when he turned up in Jerry's room Thursday night, the way he does. Peggy can't see that he ever goes home. Dale won her heart that very first night, after that meeting; he came by to see how Jerry was doing and found him wiped out, asleep, the hospital gown slipping down off his shoulders, and Peggy crouched over him on the bed, staring at him. Dale followed her eyes, looked at Jerry, at that silky black hair and the hard little path of spine, and he said to Peggy, "What a beautiful boy he is," and though she still didn't let herself cry in front of him, she felt something loosen up inside her just because of that, just because one of the doctors had finally looked at Jerry and noticed.

Now most nights he comes by and sits awhile. He doesn't examine Jerry, just comes and sits. He usually brings Doritos for Peggy, an Oreo ice cream sandwich for Jerry. He steals the sandwiches from the patient kitchen on one of the other floors; he can also get SpaghettiOs, he tells them, and all the graham crackers they want. But since Jerry doesn't eat much of anything, there doesn't seem to be a point. Sometimes he does chip away at the ice cream sandwich.

"They'll let you go with him," Dale told her. "They're used to it. They usually have both parents there. I have to warn you, though, it doesn't help the kid too much. Pain is pain."

The mean thing Peggy does is, she tells Noah he can't come in the room. He is eager to do it, to stand there with Peggy and

Jerry while the bone marrow biopsy and the spinal tap get done, and Peggy says to him, all false concern, But Noah, remember how you faint when you see blood. Tells him this in front of the oncologists, gently, sweetly, shaking her head sadly. Noah, why don't you just let me do this, since blood doesn't bother me, and you wait right here for us. Noah, honey, let's do it this way, please.

In private, with the doctors out of the room, she tells him, Noah, you walked out on your kid, you don't live with him, you're some pathetic fraction of a father. And you don't get to be there to help and comfort, that's part of what you gave up. Tough luck, fucker.

Noah gives way, wounded and resigned; she can always bulldoze him, and always could. And he does hate the sight of blood. And she is sure he will never guess the real reason she doesn't want him in the room, watching Jerry get hurt; if he sees Jerry getting hurt, he will cry, he will feel Jerry's pain, he will wish he could change places with Jerry — and if she has to watch him feeling all those things, she'll probably let the fucker move back in with her, probably discover she still loves him.

Noah, in the midst of all this, has discovered he still loves her. One night when Peggy's mother came to visit he got her to stay with Jerry, insisted on taking Peggy out for a good dinner, cozied up to her, tried to take her back to her own home. It surprised her how much she wanted to. It also made her feel guilty, with Jerry where he was. But mostly she looked at Noah and felt weary. Noah will never change. He wants to come back in her house, her care, her body, whatever. But it won't last, and it will disrupt the nicest, happiest life Peggy has ever known, herself and Jerry, alone and together. Realistically — and she tries to be nothing if not realistic — Peggy figures she has maybe nine or ten years left, before Jerry hits puberty and she loses him. Sometimes, when she wants to make herself hurt, like peeling off a scab, she makes herself think of Jerry all pimpled, Jerry drunk and throwing up, Jerry with dirty magazines, locked in the bathroom. She used to think, Well, when he gets like that, of course I won't feel the same way about him. His clean little body curled in her big lap, his hair wet from the bath. Perfect.

Now, though, she wonders. She knows that already, at four years old, he is going to stop being that perfect beautiful small boy, and so what? Of course it will make no difference to the way she feels when Jerry gets all baldheaded like the space-creature kids she sees at the hospital, with little bits of chicken fuzz on their domes. If his belly swells up and his arms and legs turn to toothpicks and he never smiles, what the hell difference will it make? And if all that won't matter, won't change how she loves him, then maybe the pimples and the drinking and the dirty magazines won't either. Maybe all teenagers have parents trailing them, like the parents who follow after in the hospital, pushing the IV poles; maybe the parents of teenagers wander along behind, loving their children the way you love a clean wet loving four-year-old.

For the day with the bone marrow biopsy and the spinal tap, Peggy wears Jerry's favorite dress, a rainbow caftan. In the treatment room she feels the doctors and the nurse looking at her; she feels enormous, a giant fat lady in multicolored gauze. They must think she is ridiculous; they must be looking at her bulk, her bright red lipstick, her somewhat unsuccessful permanent growing out, thinking she's a freak. What the hell, she doesn't give a fuck.

"Give him some more midazolam," the doctors keep saying, and the nurse puts it through the IV, and it calms Jerry down — but then they come at him with the needle, and he screams again, though in a strange weak way. The room is lined with metal shelving, boxes of medical equipment, syringes and plastic bags of IV fluid, tubes Peggy doesn't want to see. She puts her head close to Jerry's and she tells him the story of Goldilocks and the three bears. Even a week ago he would have said, No, Mama, tell me Peter Pan and the pirates. But he is slipping away from her day by day now, deeper into his safe childhood, beyond into babyhood. He says much less, and his voice is muddy, the words hard to pick out. He isn't really toilet-trained anymore, pees the bed every night. Peggy thinks that if she handed him a bottle, he would probably take it right to his mouth, though she had him trained to a cup by two and a half. For the spinal tap, he has to lie on his side, legs drawn up, fetal. She does not watch what they are doing to his back, just keeps her nose pressed close to his ear, telling the story.

The travel agency Peggy runs with her friend Marsha is not a fancy place. They book mostly budget stuff, off-season fares and packages to Caribbean hotels that need customers. They get students, retirees, lots of folks who haven't done much traveling. Often these people need help, and Peggy has a real knack for finding them the trips they want. She has never been one to let her mind drift off what she is doing, and she has never been in the habit of imagining the places she sends people. She has never been on an airplane, though at one point she and Noah covered a lot of ground in a van.

Now she thinks about travel all the time. Usually with Dale Dooley, maybe to a couples-only resort in the Bahamas, or a cruise to St. Thomas. It is sunny and she is wearing, oddly enough, her rainbow caftan. Does she expect Dale to see her the way Jerry does, oh my beautiful big mama dressed in rainbow colors? Oh god, couples only – where is Jerry?

Jerry is particularly good with crayons. It's not just that he likes drawing, which all kids do. Jerry keeps his crayons in a shoebox his father gave him, and he must have more than two hundred of them, all with the paper neatly peeled off around the worn ends. He draws for hours, big complex pictures filling pages of the oversize newsprint pads Peggy buys him, and tells her long stories: this is the dragon and he has two heads, so here are two super heroes fighting with the two different heads, and these are a bunch of lions who came to watch the fighting, but this is the king lion who has a blue crown and he is hiding behind the flower trees. She brought the box of crayons to the hospital, of course, but it seems that Jerry's drawing is melting away just like all the rest. Now he spends a long time covering the paper with careful stripes, one after another, on through his box of endless crayons. And when she asks what it is, he always tells her, A rainbow curtain. The whole page is a rainbow curtain.

The hospital kindly provides a cot, which is way too narrow for Peggy. Lying on it, she can feel her hips sliding off on both sides. So she no longer opens up the cot at night, she just takes the mattress and puts it on the floor, and most nights she takes Jerry off his bed, takes the IV along, takes his mattress down to the floor and the two of them sleep together on the two mattresses. The nurses don't like it, she can tell, but the nurses are a little scared of Peggy, she can tell.

The social worker came back and made conversation, and at the end she told Peggy, I sense you're feeling a lot of anger.

Peggy said, "Yes, I'm very angry because every day people come and stick needles into my little boy and they shoot him up with poisons."

"Well, it's really good you're able to express that," the social worker said.

Dale is one of the only people she is happy to see, maybe Dale and her mother. Her mother took the bus up that one day, stayed with Jerry, and while Noah and Peggy were out having dinner, she discovered that there was a volunteer service that would send an eager little pre-med student to your room with video games. She and Jerry played some shooting-down-rockets game all evening, and when Peggy came back, leaving behind Noah and his nonsense, her mother told her that someday Jerry should have a shirt the cobalt blue of the exploding rockets. And she had found a pizza delivery number, and Jerry had eaten most of a whole slice. The smell of pizza oil in that room comforted Peggy all night long. And even if her mother did look a little disappointed to see Peggy coming back, to see that Peggy wasn't home in bed reconciled with stupid old Noah, Peggy can understand. Her mother is as rotten a judge of manhood as Peggy herself, hates to see her daughter repeating history, wants to believe in Noah, the father of her grandchild. Peggy wants to remind her that Noah is slime, that she and Jerry are better off without him, wants to ask, Don't you think I'm doing well, was doing well until this happened? Wants to ask but doesn't; fresh from Noah's company, she knows how pathetic it looks when an adult wants to be a baby for a few hours. No way, no how. So she says, Yes, Mom, someday I'll have to find him a shirt that color.

Dale comes by at night; she doesn't know exactly why, isn't sure he does either. Dale is unhappy, she knows, sleepy and sorry for the children, sorry for himself. Dale sees her, Peggy thinks, as very tough, standing up against the hospital, fighting a battle he won't ever face. Such nonsense; she may be an ill-natured fat lady, but the hospital is Jerry's only hope; she isn't crazy or anything.

Dale has a Ph.D. in molecular genetics and he comes from a family in which everyone is a doctor. His father, his mother, two brothers, and a sister. No wonder he hates his job, Peggy supposes. Like Prince Charles, stuck in the family business. Dale has stick-out ears too. She imagines the cruise ship she just booked Mrs. Martello and her husband onto for their silver anniversary cruise. Herself and Dale doing what, exactly? Shuffleboard king and queen, no doubt.

Jerry slips further and further away, eats only mush, cries at the sight of strangers. One night Peggy tries to tell Dale how nice it was after Noah was gone and she had money coming in from her business, how all she wanted in life, really, was to sit in her own home in the evenings with someone she loved this much, someone so small and so perfect. Jerry's personality has always seemed big enough to fill the house, as big as any other person's. Now in the hospital it is clear that it is little, a child-size work of art, disappearing, fading before her eyes. She imagines that when the doctors (except Dale) think about Jerry, they see only the malignant cells in the bone marrow, dividing and taking over all the space where Jerry's blood is made. They see the chemotherapy attacking, like the rockets' red glare. Like the video game. Zap. But now sometimes she catches herself thinking of Jerry that way, A Kid With Cancer. What else is left? Urinal, bedpan, blood draw. He screams when he sees the blood techs. Lunch tray, blood pressure. Taking a walk down the hall, pushing his pole, he sees a bald kid and starts crying. Does he know that she is starting to find webs of hair on his pillow?

Dale brings some syringes and needles to the room one night after a particularly bad day. Peggy was crying secretly but is afraid he can see tear tracks, so goes off to wash her face. Comes back to find Dale holding out his arm, saying, Go ahead, do it. Jerry stabs the needle into Dale's arm, wild glee on his face such as Peggy has not seen in days and days. Again, Dale says. Here's another needle. Go ahead. He looks up at Peggy and says in extenuation, I only brought small needles. Jerry could go on with this all night. There is nothing babyish about the malice in his face, the joy of jabbing those needles into the doctor.

That night Jerry talks a little more, asks some of the questions he's given up asking: How long will I be sick, will I get better, when can we go home? Soon, Peggy promises him, to our own house, our very own, with no nurses and no doctors. Except maybe, could Doctor Dale come and visit sometimes?

She remembers the night Dale came to tell her that the studies on the bone marrow were finished, that Jerry has the "good kind" of leukemia, the common kind that has the highest rate of cure. Ninety percent or so. And after only a couple of days, she was already delighted to hear there was only a one-in-ten chance Jerry would be dead soon. Only one in ten. They'll tell you all about it tomorrow, Dale said, but I thought I'd stick around and let you know tonight. He wandered off, into his own life, which Peggy has little energy to imagine, and she took Jerry by the shoulders, looked in his eyes, said, Did you hear that? You're going to get better, you little runt.

She holds him at night and feels his breathing, his heart beating in his tiny birdcage chest, senses him all night long like a mother with a new baby who worries about crib death. She thinks about a trip to a resort she cannot quite identify, hot sun baking down on little whitewashed bungalows with rounded windows, set along paths through a grove of palm trees. She walks there alone, no Jerry, no Noah, no Dale, no other people at all.

They will go home, finally, when Jerry has enough white blood cells. Every morning they wait for the number to come back. When he has a count of more than five hundred, he can go home and start coming to the oncology clinic once a week. In her mind, Peggy puts her house back in order; dirty laundry dumped here and there, newspapers still folded, unread, dust and confusion. It won't take long to clean it up. It won't take long to have Jerry back to drawing his big pictures, to buy him a new newsprint pad. She holds him at night and feels his breathing, and she whispers in his ear too softly to wake him, I will show you what is behind the rainbow curtain.

Necessary Risks

TO TELL THE TRUTH, Caroline is more than a little cynical about this whole dude-ranch male-bonding thing. To tell the truth, she feels like saying to her husband, Wait a minute, this whole second-child thing was your idea. To tell the truth, she wants out.

But she has no way out. How does a mother pooh-pooh the idea that her husband and her son want some special time together, some manhood back-to-nature really *really* talking time? How does she turn her cynical and grouchy and selfish tones on their two-week trip to ride trails and fish mountain rivers and make boy-conversation under the stars? How can she not be touched that they want to do this thing, by a fourteen-year-old who would rather be in the great outdoors with his father than in the video arcades with his friends for the last weeks of the summer, by a mild-mannered mathematician who is willing to sit on a horse for the first time in his life to indulge this father-son fantasy. Okay, Caroline is touched. Okay, she's moved. Okay, she recognizes that she has a kind and loving child in Gary, a worthy and generous husband in Steve.

And I love my daughter, I do. Body and mind and soul, I love her. But please, don't leave me alone with her for two weeks. She's not what you'd call easy. *I'm* not what you'd call easy. We'll never make it. We exist in a nice balance, mother and daughter, but only because we aren't left alone together. I don't do well with noise and disorder and destruction, and Emilie thrives on them. We wear each other out, we bring out the worst in each other, and of course it's my fault, since she's the four-year-old and I'm the grownup. Jesus, Steve, what if she doesn't love me anymore by the time you come back, not after all the fighting and yelling? Steve, we need a cushion, we need your easygoing presence.

Pull your socks up, Caroline. You're the grownup here.

She is doing the anesthesia for a gall bladder removal today; the guy is overweight but otherwise in pretty good shape, doesn't smoke or anything. The surgeon is one of her favorites; plays classical music in the operating room, remembers to say please, works quickly, has a low complications rate. This operation is a good bet to go smoothly, and Caroline is not looking ahead to any problems. But then she goes in to check the patient one more time before surgery, and overnight he seems to have developed a miserable cold. His eyes are watering, his nose is running, and when he sits up in the hospital bed so she can listen to his chest, he starts coughing.

In spite of all that, he's mad at her when she tells him, "I think we're going to have to postpone your surgery." If you were a really good doctor, she can see he is thinking, if you were really good, you wouldn't have any problems anesthetizing me even if I do have a cold. What's a little cold, anyway?

"You see, sir," Caroline says firmly, "this isn't an emergency operation. It's an operation that was planned and scheduled and can easily be rescheduled. And there's no reason to take any unnecessary risks."

No reason to take any unnecessary risks. Life is full of necessary risks, after all; later this morning she's scheduled to do the anesthesia for an endarterectomy, an operation to clean out the clogged neck artery of a rather frail elderly woman. Dicey heart, compromised blood supply — those are necessary risks. There's no way to avoid them and still get the surgery done. And the truth is, though Caroline is a very careful and talented doctor, though she will sit for an hour trying to foresee every conceivable problem with a particular patient, a particular operation, though she is, like most anesthesiologists, a total control freak, she also lives for those moments when something goes wrong. You avoid all unnecessary risks, you control all controllable factors, and then every once in a while the patient's blood pressure drops all the way down or the heart stops or there's an idiosyncratic reaction to one of the anesthetic drugs and the temperature rockets up — and those are the moments when you find out how good you are. And Caroline is very, very good.

She lets the surgeons know about the gall bladder case, the upper respiratory infection. The next case will be moved up to use the operating room, so she goes and sits in her little cubicle of an office, stares at the framed pictures of Gary, Emilie, Steve. This damn-fool dude-ranch idea. This taking off together and leaving her at home with the second child, with the daughter. Talk about unnecessary risks of one kind or another! Two city boys out on big horses. A mother and her four-year-old daughter alone together for two weeks. Having a second child really was Steve's idea. Gary was born right after Caroline finished medical school. She had energy and drive and also, of course, a husband who spent his days at home in a tiny study, working on his Ph.D. Caroline kept on schedule, even though at moments she thought it was going to kill her; Steve took an extra year to finish his dissertation. Don't worry, he said. It'll be better for the extra time. Meanwhile, there's no reason to assume I'll be able to get a job as a math professor; better to have you ready to support us. Anesthesiologists get jobs.

So she finished, and indeed she got a job and supported him

happily and reasonably lavishly through a couple of years when he could get only skimpy fellowships, and then, when he took a teaching job he hated at a local technical college, she went so far as to encourage him to quit. You need time to work on your own stuff, she said, though she understood nothing of his own stuff. It didn't matter; she believed. She still believes, though that's easier now; he did take a couple of years and work on his own weird abstruse un-understandable stuff, and he was rewarded with a real job, and with a promotion. And then, when Gary was almost ten years old, he came up with this idea about a second child. In fact, Emilie is named for an eighteenth-century mathematician, the marquise du Chatelet, Voltaire's brilliant mistress, the woman who helped translate Isaac Newton's *Principia Mathematica* into French.

Here they are, neatly lined up on her desk. Gary is a tall and unexpectedly graceful fourteen now, and Steve has tenure and a certain standing in his field. He and Caroline are trapped, she sometimes thinks, in those identities they chose back when Gary was little; she is still driven and disciplined and prone to plotting out every single minute, and he is loose and gentle and a little bit distracted, the way he was with his baby all those years ago. We have all the time in the world, says Steve's benignly absent-minded demeanor. Let's enjoy watching time slip by. Seconds count, Caroline imagines would be her own motto, and the thing is, of course, in her job they do.

The elderly woman who is going in for the endarterectomy is terrified. She hadn't been expecting such an early summons to the operating room, and she seems to feel that this change in schedule is sinister and suggestive of larger disorders, larger dangers. Caroline listens carefully to her heart, her lungs. The woman clutches at her neck, thinking no doubt of the clogged-up artery that has betrayed her into this danger, the carotid, which should be supplying her brain with copious oxygen-rich blood and is instead in constant danger of sealing off altogether: stroke, darkness, death.

"You're in great shape, just terrific," Caroline tells this frail and pale woman, so anonymous in her yellow hospital gown. She makes her voice firm and confident and almost congratulatory: How lucky you are to be well enough to have this operation, which will help you so much, how lucky you are to have me for your anesthesiologist. When the lights are about to go out, Caroline believes, people want promises: I'll be there with you, everything's fine, it'll be morning soon, of course you won't die.

"Will you be there the whole time?" The woman struggles into a partial sitting position, resting on her elbows, looking searchingly into Caroline's professional, reassuring face with her own unfaded, unhesitant, jade-green eyes.

The morning Steve and Gary are due to leave for the dude ranch, Caroline is watching her easily distracted husband sort clean laundry into a duffel bag. Nothing is folded, socks are unpaired. Gary has taken possession of the list of suggested clothes — this really is like some demented sleep-away camp; it's surprising they don't want iron-on name labels. Anyway, Gary is upset that his father hasn't planned more carefully, hasn't bought the water-resistant rain pants for them both, or even the special high-potency bug repellant. Mildly, cheerfully, Steve suggests that everything will surely be available out where they're going. Caroline, sitting in female solidarity with Emilie on the couch and watching the proceedings, is of course aware that if she, Caroline, the control freak, did happen to be going to a dude ranch, she would naturally have gone down the list systematically, checking off each and every item, and with days to spare. So maybe, she thinks, Gary gets his chromosomes but my temperament, Emilie gets the extra X and her father's lack of organization. Very neat; Mother and Dad and Sis and Chip; he has my freckles, she has your curls.

Ha. Gary is his own blend of emerging adolescence and reaction to his parents, and Emilie . . . well, Emilie must be regarded as the creature from the black lagoon. A force of nature. To prove the point, Emilie hops off the sofa. She does not move delicately; she never moves delicately. She is the lightest, smallest person in the family, a sturdy forty inches or so, and yet the house shakes when she walks. A solid round girl with a dark-brown bowl haircut, what they used to call a Dutch bob, Emilie has her own way of occupying space; it is as if she has spent her whole life compensating for being so much smaller and so much lighter than everyone else.

"I am going to pack my own suitcase," she announces. After a minute of energetic bustling, she has two paper shopping bags standing open in the middle of the living room and is busily selecting her clothes out of Steve's laundry basket. And always, as always, in every possible way, she creates mess and chaos. The shopping bags are dragged out of the newspaper recycling pile; old newspapers are strewn across the floor. Plus, one of the shopping bags had some flour spilled in the bottom; that's the one into which she's throwing her clean underpants by the handful. Every time she snatches clothes from the basket, other clothes come with them and drop by the wayside. Gary and Steve seem models of packing propriety by comparison. And of course she's singing. She's always singing. She is very loud; she has no problems projecting that voice. She is intermittently tuneful. And her style of songwriting is relatively consistent.

> "Packing up my suitcase,
> I am packing up my snootcase,
> I am packing up my dootcase,
> I am packing up my gootcase . . ."

Conversation is impossible. Caroline is not going to tell her to lower her voice. She is not going to tell her to put the clean laundry back in the basket. Ordinarily that would be Caroline's role; she sometimes worries that her entire relationship with her daughter is one long string of requests for less noise, less mess, less chaos. When she reads one of those articles about how girls lose their self-confidence and stop speaking up for themselves right around puberty, she always has a guilty pang: Emilie, all grown up, sitting in a therapist's office explaining, "My mother, she was always telling me to talk more softly." Then again, Caroline does not believe that she herself ever went through that loss of confidence, so why should Emilie, who seems to have enough confidence to supply the power needs of a small midwestern city?

Emilie finds a new and irresistible twist to make her packing that much more exciting. She stands across the living room and throws books and toys in the general direction of the shopping bags, screaming with joy when a well-flung harmonica actually falls inside a bag.

"Emilie, stop throwing things." It is finally Steve, her father, who has to squelch her; he has just been hit in the jaw by a Hot Wheels car.

Hee-hee. Caroline for once is enjoying her daughter's havoc. Take that, you would-be cowboy, you. Run for safety, head for the hills.

And they do. They phone for a cab and load their duffels into the trunk and off they go. Caroline hugs her son, kisses her husband with one of those passionate, what-if-we-never-meet-again farewell embraces in which nobody actually explicitly thinks about plane crashes, and waves as the taxi drives down the street. For a moment she has successfully vanquished her worst self and is cheering the father-son endeavor: Have a great time, guys! Unfortunately, just as the cab is lost to sight, Emilie experimentally spins in a circle, firing a handful of pebbles as she goes. One hits her mother in the side and another, with uncanny accuracy, breaks the sideview mirror on the next-door neighbor's new Acura, safely parked in its own driveway.

This has not ever been Caroline's job. She does not do Emilie in the morning. She normally leaves for work long before the other members of her family are really awake; anesthesiology, like surgery, is an early-morning enterprise. She is accustomed to picking Emilie up at the end of the day-care day, to Emilie when she is a little, just a little, worn out by a full day of making messes, authorized and unauthorized, running wild in the playground, bouncing off fifteen other four-year-olds. That has always been the mother-daughter time together; late afternoon, come home, kick your shoes off, maybe think about dinner. Mornings belong to Steve.

"Mom forgot my lunchbox,
My bunchbox,
My crunchbox!"

Emilie, who has recently burst the bounds of her car seat, sits happily in the back seat and sings. Sings good and loud, needless to say; her voice is amplified by the small enclosed space. And Caroline, who is on the edge of a really loud reprimand, on the edge of shouting, "Don't you ever sing in the car again!" suddenly surprises herself by taking a deep breath and singing almost as loudly as her daughter.

"Mom had to drive back for your lunchbox,
Your bunchbox, your crunchbox,
Mom had to drive back for your lunchbox,
And now she is gonna be late!"

Emilie swings the lunchbox in question as hard as she can and hits her mother in the back of the head.

"Don't sing when I am singing!" she orders, so then, of course, Caroline does have to let loose after all and scream, "I might have crashed the car, don't you ever do that again, put that lunchbox down on the floor and don't even touch it till we get there!"

"Awoo! Awoo!" howls Emilie, deep crazy-making call-of-the-wild wolf howls; she keeps them up, naturally, all the way to day care, then interrupts her heartbroken cries to whisper smugly, just loud enough so her mother can hear, "Actually, I was still touching my lunchbox all the way."

Every damn morning is some version of this. And the afternoons, which used to be their pleasant time together, are poisoned, Caroline thinks, because she is still secretly mad about the mornings. And mad that in order to make time for these horrible mornings, she has gone to great lengths to abbreviate her schedule, letting other anesthesiologists sub for her at important operations and feeling guilty about it.

She stomps into her office with wholly unaccustomed vehemence. Slams down her briefcase on the desk and watches as it knocks off a pencil holder, an ugly little contraption Gary made for her when he was in third or fourth grade, tiny colored tiles glued onto a coffee can. Gary, my sweet, good, easy boy, I'm sorry. She bends to pick up the coffee can; several tiles have come off, and she gathers them up tenderly. Then straightens and hits her head hard on the corner of the desk. Sinks into her chair and rubs her head. Oh, Emilie, my little girl, I'm sorry, but I just can't do this. Oh, my sweet, darling, determined little monster from hell, this is making me hate you. This is making me hate myself. And making me act like not myself; look at me, I'm knocking things over and banging my head — why, I'm acting like you.

Pull yourself together, girl. Caroline takes a tissue from the box on her desk and delicately, deliberately, blows her nose. She recognizes herself as a mass of unfamiliar sensations; she feels guilty at work about not coming in as early as usual, she feels incompetent and helpless in the morning when she deals with her daughter, she feels lonely without Steve. Guilty, incompetent, lonely — well, she tells herself grimly, this should be pretty educational. A brand-new way of looking at yourself, a brand-new perspective.

Her beeper goes off. An emergency operation; the schedule is being changed. There's a kid down in the emergency room with a ruptured appendix, looks pretty sick. Please go pre-op him right away; the breast reconstruction she was expecting to do won't happen till the afternoon.

And the kid in the emergency room does indeed look pretty sick. His name is Jordan; he's eight years old. Jordan's mother is sitting by his bedside, staring helplessly at the IV bottle, the monitor, the lines. Jordan is groaning in pain, his face pale, sweat on his forehead. Caroline pulls up a stainless steel stool next to the mother and notices how young she looks, this mother of an eight-year-old. She's tiny, with a little puff of blond hair, and she's wearing denim shorts and a big loose sweatshirt with a cartoon cat on it. She looks twelve or thirteen; because of the sweatshirt, you can't see whether she has breasts, and her face is unlined and tear-stained.

Caroline introduces herself. "I'll be doing the anesthesia for Jordan's surgery, so I need to ask you some questions and examine him — "

The blond woman cuts her off. "I swear to God, I didn't know it was this," she says.

"Of course you didn't. These things take everyone by surprise. Now, has Jordan basically been a pretty healthy kid?"

"He's never had anything, nothing's ever been wrong. I swear to God!" She reaches over and adjusts the sheet over her son, and Caroline takes the opportunity to lean across the counter and snag a hospital-issue box of tissues, has it ready to offer.

"Does Jordan have any allergies to any medications?" Look, she wants to say, I'm not bothering you just because I'm a meanie. I know you're upset. But in half an hour I'm going to be controlling the beating of your son's heart and the air in his lungs, and you have to help me do it right.

"He doesn't have any problems! He can eat anything he wants, not like his cousin – she's allergic to raspberries and strawberries, and if there's peanut butter in a cookie it might kill her. Jordan isn't allergic to anything! So naturally when he had this stomachache we thought it must just be some little bug – and then it got worse and worse all day, and I swear to God we were going to take him to the hospital last night, and then all of a sudden it stopped hurting, and we thought, see, it was just a bug, it's going away – "

"That happens sometimes," Caroline says, as soothingly as she can. "Sometimes when the appendix gets inflamed and it's really hurting, it goes on to rupture, and the pain gets better because the pressure is relieved. But as I'm sure the doctors down here have already explained, that makes it even more important to do the operation right away, so I need to know whether Jordan is allergic to any *medications*. Has he ever had a bad reaction to any drug he was taking? Penicillin? Anything else?"

She cannot totally keep the urgency out of her voice; she is imagining the bacteria from the ruptured appendix spreading throughout the usually sterile cavities of Jordan's abdomen. Peritonitis, overwhelming infection, shock.

In fact, it's a rotten, dirty operation, takes much longer than the usual appendectomy, and Caroline worries all the way through that she's going to lose the boy. He is already close to slipping into shock, and as she listens to the surgeons, exclaiming as they explore the abdomen, she thinks of the hurried exam she did down in the emergency room, the boy's belly rigid under her touch.

At one point, after the operation has been going on for a while, Jordan's blood pressure starts to slip downward. Caroline changes the dosages, sends drugs into his lines to kick his heart a little, tighten down his blood vessels and bring up the pressure. A little more fluid, a soft-voiced but compelling request to the blood bank to send up some blood. Normally a kid doesn't need blood transfusions during an appendectomy, but this is taking too long, he's probably losing more blood than most, and if he goes into shock he might start chewing up his red cells.

The chief surgeon looks up at her, and their eyes meet over their surgical masks. "His pressure's dropping, Joe," she says. "I don't like the way he looks. How much longer are you gonna need?"

"We're getting ready to close up," says the surgeon.

Caroline is worried about losing the boy. She doesn't think consciously about his mother, about the tiny blond woman sitting out in the family waiting area working her way through one box of tissues after another, or maybe praying, or maybe even taking her turn at the pay phone and telling someone or other over and over how she thought it was some kind of stomach bug. But the mother is there, somewhere on Caroline's shoulder, and everyone who taught her is there, and everyone whose heart and lungs she has taken over for a few hours is there, a great cloud of them, like the cloud of faces with God when he gives life to Adam on the Sistine Chapel ceiling. Yes, go ahead and call it playing God if you want; what other word is there for this responsibility? I breathe for him, I send the gases into his lungs through a tube that I have carefully positioned in the right place. I kick his heart and make it beat, I fill his blood vessels with fluid and tighten them down if they don't adjust themselves, I give him new blood if he doesn't have enough of his own. There is a certain element of mysticism to it all, despite the gleaming, beeping machines and monitors, and perhaps even a certain sense of transubstantiation: We are one body, you and I.

All of which is to say that though she is worried about Jordan, though she is conscious of his waiting mother and her terror, Caroline would rather be right here right now than anywhere else on earth. This is her right and proper place, this is what she knows how to do. And when the surgeons have finished closing, when she has successfully avoided the blood transfusion she thought he was going to need, when she is watching with pleasure as his pressure and heart rate stabilize, she feels some mixture of pride and gratitude, thrill and satisfaction.

"I took care of a boy today who had a very, very bad stomachache," she says to Emilie that afternoon as they walk together out of the day-care center. Caroline is carrying the lunchbox of discord, also Emilie's green sweatshirt, also three large collages of macaroni and fingerpaint on corrugated cardboard. Emilie is carrying, with great tenderness and attention, a wilting dandelion that she found in the playground and nursed all afternoon in a paper cup of water. Caroline is not wild about the idea of cups of water in the car, but she isn't going to make a big thing about it. She is full of good resolutions, mixed up peculiarly with images of Jordan waking up slowly in the pediatric intensive care unit with his parents sitting by his bed, that tiny mother, that unexpectedly graying, distinguished, executive father.

"Why did he have a very, very bad stomachache?"

"Something in his stomach called his appendix was making him sick."

"Did he throw up?" asks Emilie, who is prone to violent, even volcanic stomach upsets herself, usually after dietary indiscretions.

"He did throw up. And his stomach hurt him a lot."

"Sometimes *I* throw up and then you take care of *me*."

Caroline straps her daughter into the car as Emilie carefully holds the cup of water aloft. Avoid unnecessary risks, Caroline is thinking, and drives home particularly slowly and gently, so that Emilie doesn't spill even a drop.

"Rebecca's father had a very bad stomachache one time and he almost died," says Emilie that night as they eat dinner. "Did the boy at your hospital almost died?"

Caroline feels a sudden shot of pride, a kick to the heart. Those complex sentences, the struggle to get the words right, to express ideas that are not simple. And the memory; *Hours go by, and Emilie is still thinking about something we talked about on the ride home.*

"Well," she says diplomatically, "he was very, very sick with his stomachache, but we made him better."

Even though in her bath Emilie becomes rambunctious and manages to soak not only the bathroom floor but also her mother's towel, which is hanging all the way across the room, which suggests not only water splashed but water deliberately thrown, and even though Caroline opens the lunchbox to make tomorrow's lunch and discovers that all three little plastic containers and the thermos have lost their lids, she is still able to be cheerful when Steve calls from the dude ranch. I'm glad it's fun, I'm glad Gary likes the riding. Don't worry about us, buckaroos, we're doing just fine.

Caroline has been dreading the weekend just a little bit. Two days of only Emilie and her. By next weekend the guys will be back. The initial idea was to set up something for Emilie to do;

maybe her friend Rebecca can come over. But it's one of those last weekends of the summer, and everyone is gone – Rebecca and her family, Emilie's other best friend and her family. It's gonna be you and me, kid, Caroline tells her sleeping daughter on Saturday morning. Good, let her sleep. Maybe we should have made plans, maybe we should have gone away ourselves. Thinking of last night's phone call from the dude ranch: great trout fishing, perfect weather, Gary fell off a horse but he's fine. But here the weather is rotten, Caroline consoles herself, looking out the window at gray skies and dull, heavy air.

Rotten, it turns out, is not the word. In this state, which never gets hurricanes, there is a hurricane watch. It's all anyone can talk about on the radio, this unexpected swerve in the path of a storm way out at sea, now heading straight for this usually protected section of the North Atlantic coast. When Emilie comes downstairs, shaggy and sleep-sated, Caroline is watching the local news special on TV: stock up on candles, bottled water, flashlights. Put masking tape on exposed windows. Lay in a stock of food that does not require cooking or refrigeration. The camera keeps cutting to the local weatherman, a gangly stork of a fellow who looks as if a hurricane would snap him in two; he has a big map up and is tracking the progress of the storm. Hurricane Harriet, now so many miles off the coast of, moving at a speed of, expected to strike land later this afternoon. Now we take you to an interview with the local chief of police: stay off the roads, keep the emergency phone lines clear.

Caroline is not very alarmed by all this, but when Emilie is dressed and ready for action, the two of them do walk down the block to buy some groceries and flashlight batteries. The store is out of batteries, every kind of battery, making Caroline wonder whether people are loading up their calculators and their digital watches against the coming storm. The grocery, a small neighborhood store, is jammed with people who are stuffing their shopping baskets with canned goods, plastic bags of pretzels and corn chips. There is a genuine atmosphere of panic, to Caroline's surprise, and for a minute she almost catches the bug: Oh, my God, no bottled water! What will we do? But Caroline is schooled to be calm in moments of general panic, and as she allows Emilie to fill their shopping cart with exuberant slam-dunks of macaroni, cereal, and chocolate syrup, she is thinking, What we'll do is, we'll go home and fill some bottles with the perfectly good water that comes out of the tap — that's what we'll do.

She fills the bottles and even the bathtub, she cooks up a couple of pounds of macaroni, which Emilie can happily eat at every meal, and then she takes her daughter in her lap and they watch a little more of the television coverage. The day outside has become peculiarly dark, and the wind is rising, and Caroline no longer feels quite as silly as she did when she filled the bathtub. It does feel a little ominous now, the darkening day, the warnings of death and destruction. However, there is something undeniably cozy about battening down, mother and daughter, in their sturdy house, which has stood on its street, a good thirty miles in from the sea, for at least a hundred years. There are worse places to be. They play a game of Chinese checkers; they eat grilled cheese sandwiches for lunch. Let the storm rage, Caroline thinks, enjoying the mix of boredom and excitement of this dark and fierce day, these calm domestic hours. She turns on the news once again.

Emilie cannot sit and watch television for very long, especially boring television with talking adults and closeups of maps. She is up and running soon, and as Caroline sits watching, she hears the unmistakable splash of something large and heavy falling into the filled bathtub. Immediately she is up on her feet, rushing to rescue her daughter, whom she finds standing high and dry on the toilet seat amid the floodwaters. What she has thrown into the tub is her brother's saxophone, in its heavy black case.

Caroline takes a deep breath, thinking in some part of her orderly list-making mind, *Rescue saxophone, clean floor, lose temper, refill tub* . . . but the phone rings and her beeper, left behind in the kitchen, beeps faintly, all at the same moment.

"What the hell?" she says out loud. Rescues the saxophone, drops a towel on the floor, and goes to answer the phone.

"What the hell?" she says to the obstetrician. "I'm not on call this weekend. My husband's away, I've got my daughter – I made sure I wasn't on call."

"You're on call for the disaster system," he tells her. "Just like me. We're the ones who live closest, the ones who can get here if there's a natural disaster – like this hurricane. And we need you."

Caroline is only very dimly aware of the disaster system. It has never, to her knowledge, been invoked before in the ten years she has worked at this hospital. But here is the obstetrician telling her that all the major roads have been closed, that the police are waving down motorists and sending them home, and that the police are even now on their way to pick her up and take her to the hospital. Then he cuts himself off in midsentence and rushes away, without telling her why they need her. An emergency cesarean, she supposes; the in-house anesthesiologist must be busy with something else.

When the police arrive, sirens screaming, there is of course no point at all in suggesting that they detour to take Emilie to a babysitter's house. Emilie is actually awed by the noise and lights and fast driving and clings to her mother as some timid, gentle four-year-old might do. All around them are tree limbs on the road, and the wind howls so loudly that Caroline can hear it through the window whenever the siren noise dips slightly in between crescendos.

When Caroline gets to the hospital, they fill her in. A bad case, a rotten case, an emergency. A couple driving along, the husband driving, the wife, almost eight months pregnant, sitting beside him. Right at the beginning of the windstorm but out toward the coast, where the wind's been much worse. Didn't listen to the news reports, didn't know they weren't supposed to be driving. A bad accident, a tree limb crashing down across the car, another car plowing into them. One of those freak things: the husband walks away with a couple of scratches; the wife wasn't wearing her seatbelt – multiple trauma to the head and chest, neck broken, head bashed in, brain swelling up. She's not going to make it. The EMTs have basically been coding her ever since they found her. The neurosurgeons have already tried. Fact is, they would probably have pronounced her dead if not for the baby. They've been keeping her alive in intensive care, but it's touch and go. The husband finally said, Okay, go ahead and take the baby.

Emilie has been left with one of the nurses, who is also helping out in the recovery room. "I'm sorry," Caroline manages to murmur in passing, but her mind is already in the operating room, and so is the nurse's. The operating rooms and recovery rooms are busy; this isn't the only automobile accident of the day. Just the worst one, the one that has every doctor and every nurse thinking, Imagine if that were me, if that were my wife, my baby.

As a technical challenge for an anesthesiologist, it is complex but without any joy. Caroline cranks up her miracle drugs, pushing this woman's heart as far as it will go. Is anything getting to the brain at all? Who knows, but Caroline pushes painkillers as well, just in case, and even finds herself, as the surgery starts, leaning over and whispering into the clean pink ear of this unknown woman, "They're going to take your baby out now, dear, you're going to have your baby, and your baby's going to be fine."

Who knows, after all; there are lots of studies that suggest that people in comas sometimes hear something, respond to something, remember something. Caroline smooths the straight black hair off the woman's cheek. Most of her head is swathed in bandages. Linda Flanagan, that's her name. They had the anesthesia history all done when she arrived, must have gotten it from the husband. Linda Flanagan, previously healthy, twenty-seven years old, no known allergies, thirty-three weeks pregnant, normal pregnancy.

It's a tense and rapid, almost silent cesarean section, here in the operating room, where no sound of the hurricane can penetrate, where the weather, with all its blind destructiveness, is irrelevant and far away. They don't waste any time trying for the smallest possible incision; they cut a big, old-fashioned incision. Caroline gives blood and more blood; this lady is losing it fast. The obstetrician pulls out the baby with that unmistakable wet sucking sound of the body giving up its own. Caroline waits, everyone waits, for the baby to cry. Sounds of suction, sounds of gentle hands slapping on a wet body as the nurses attend to the newborn. Caroline bends to her own work: push the heart, fill the vessels. "You have a girl, Linda," she whispers. "Congratulations." She thinks, irresistibly, of her own delivery room, of Emilie's birth, of the congratulations and the feel of the blanket-wrapped body in her arms, already so very definitely Emilie and no one else. She hopes Emilie is okay, worries suddenly and fiercely that Emilie is not okay, and it is only when the weak cries of a premature and badly stressed newborn float across the tiled operating room that she relaxes, smiles through her mask at the obstetricians, who have both, in unison, pumped jubilant clenched fists at the ceiling. So that was why I was worrying about Emilie, she thinks, understanding.

In fact, of all things, of all totally bizarre and inappropriate things, when Caroline has transferred her patient back to the intensive care unit doctor and goes looking for her daughter, she finds her in the family waiting room, guarded and watched by Linda Flanagan's husband. An emergency in the recovery room, a day when the staff is way down — the nurse had to do what she could.

"I'm so sorry," Caroline says to Mr. Flanagan, a plump, friendly-looking young man with small bandages on his forehead, his hand, his ear. What is she apologizing for? For the insanity of making him baby-sit while his wife has surgery, while his child is delivered. For the storm, raging outside now with a force that shakes the double-glazed unopenable hospital windows in the waiting room. For the branch, for the accident, for his wife's death.

Actually, it looks more than a little like the hurricane has hit the inside of the waiting room, and knowing her daughter, Caroline has no doubt about the reason all the chairs have been stripped of their cushions, all the cushions piled into a barricade across the floor. Chairs are upside down at either end, and other chairs are tipped over and scattered here and there. Every towel has been pulled out of the paper towel dispenser by the sink and carefully flattened out, and they have been arranged in a ring around the wall of cushions and chairs. The coffee filters have been removed from the cabinet under the coffee machine, opened into little round tents, and placed at intervals around the ring of paper towels. And paper cups filled with water stand here and there around the floor, like the one Caroline has just kicked over. She feels dazzled and exhausted by her daughter: talk about destructive force. Emilie is the queen of the disaster system.

"I'm so sorry," she says again to Mr. Flanagan, and then, when he seems about to mop up the water she spilled, she reaches past him, grabs a paper towel or two, and does it herself.

"No! No! You're wrecking my fort!" Emilie comes thundering across the floor, cannons into her mother as she bends, and actually succeeds in knocking her over, right into the spilled water. Mr. Flanagan reaches down a hand to help her up, but then, as she takes it, he changes his mind and sinks down onto the floor beside her. Caroline, wet through her pants, looks at his gentle bandaged face and reaches out to gather her daughter close, squeeze her tight.

"You have a daughter," she says. "I guess you know."

"You do?" Emilie asks with interest. "I didn't know that. Is she as big as me?"

"No," he says. "She's just a little baby right now. But I hope someday she'll be as big and strong as you are."

"I'm so sorry," Caroline says yet again, this time knowing exactly what she means.

"At least I had your daughter to watch while I was waiting," Mr. Flanagan says, and now the tears are running frankly down his nose. "That helped a lot."

"We made a fort! I did most of it!" Emilie does not seem particularly disturbed that her new friend is crying.

"When you watch her, you know," Mr. Flanagan says, nodding his head at Emilie, "somehow you just have to believe that life goes on." And he buries his head in his hands and cries the way people cry when they understand that a certain life will not go on after all.

"I'm sorry," Caroline says, pressing her face into Emilie's hair.

Emilie, who is, after all, quite wise in the ways of crying and being comforted, pats first her mother's shoulder and then Mr. Flanagan's. "It's okay," she tells them. "Don't cry, your eyes will get all red. It's okay. You can come in my fort."

They make their way across the floor, through the cups of water and the coffee filters and across the moat of paper towels, to sit on the cushions and listen to the wind, waiting for someone to come get Mr. Flanagan and take him to say hello to his daughter or goodbye to his wife. When the nurse from the newborn intensive care unit does come to the door and he gets up to go, he says courteously to Emilie, "Thank you for making that great fort."

"You're welcome," says Emilie.

"Thank you for everything you've done, doctor," he says to Caroline. He shakes her hand quickly and then he's gone, leaving her sitting on the cushions and holding tight to her daughter until she squirms away.

Intimacy

"WE FINALLY got to do it last night," Joyce confides. Joyce and Eddie have been seeing an intimacy counselor to work out problems in their four-month-old relationship. Apparently people don't break up anymore. The intimacy counselor has had them on an Intimacy Exploration Program. One night they had to take off their clothes and lie in bed naked, not touching, while discussing their first summers at camp. Another night they had to give each other backrubs, blindfolded. But they have not been allowed to have intercourse, which has been a strain, since, according to Joyce, that is one thing they do pretty well together.

Joyce is dissecting a dead salad. I am eating blueberry yogurt. According to the counselor, Joyce and Eddie both have severe intimacy problems. Joyce has explained to me (the counselor having explained it to her) that though she thinks she *wants* a long-term relationship, she is actually *afraid* of intimacy, and so she becomes controlling. And when Joyce becomes controlling, she continues (the counselor continued), well, this really pushes all of Eddie's buttons.

The obvious question for me to ask now is, "Well, was it different after all the Intimacy Exploration?" I keep spooning up my blueberry yogurt. The teachers' lunchroom is fairly noisy, with Mr. Gruber, who runs the computer center, enticing two of the sensitive young male teachers to contribute nasty ethnic jokes for a collection he swears he is putting together. Actually he is trying to undermine everything the Pleasant Meadows School stands for: upper-middle-class ethnic diversity and a profound respect for the arts and crafts of persecuted Third World peoples, combined with high SAT scores and 25 percent Ivy League placements every year.

"It's hard to say, of course," Joyce goes on. "I mean, after we didn't do it for such a long time, I guess it was bound to seem more special when we finally did. But I do think we got through some important barriers. I think that even if we don't exactly have the same intimacy agenda yet, we at least know that we're both searching together, you know what I mean?"

Intimacy counseling has made Joyce into a lousy friend. Instead of gossiping about her love life, which used to brighten up my lunch hour, I have to hear this gibberish. Needless to say, the counselor has helped her to focus more closely on *her* needs and *her* problems, so she never asks me anything about myself. I am nearly dead with fatigue today, which is probably making me more impatient; this morning I got into the car after dropping my five-month-old off at the day-care center and sat there, dull and stupid, afraid to begin driving because my vision seemed oily and thick. So I started the car and switched on the radio, hoping a little music would get me going. On the radio, Murray the Morning Man and Sweet Sue were carrying on one of their contests; they were about to choose a postcard out of the magic barrel and give some lucky listener the chance to win a five-day trip to Barbados. For maybe ten seconds, sitting in that parking lot with the empty baby car seat next to me, I really believed they were going to call my name. I knew just what they'd say, just what I would have to do. "You have twenty minutes to call us and say the magic words: Murray and Sue, I listen to you, on one-oh-two! Call us up, say the magic words, and the trip to Barbados is yours!" I felt in my coat pocket and found some change.

The trip went to someone named Chuck Finster, from Quincy. Lucky Chuck. Of course, he had actually sent in a postcard and entered the contest, which was more than I had done. I started the car and drove to work, thinking all the time about the trip to Barbados, about a plastic hotel room and tacky tropical drinks. It sounded good. The trip was for two, of course, and I wondered whether old Chuck had anyone to take, anyone he could carry away from Boston in December. By the time I got to Pleasant Meadows, it was sleeting.

I have to say this about Joyce: she is a damn good teacher. She teaches the most popular English electives in the school, one on fantasy literature for the tenth-graders, which attracts all the sword-and-sorcery computer nerd boys, and she nudges them right along until they find themselves reading Poe and LeFanu and Robert Louis Stevenson, and another course on women's literature, in which they don't read a single author who committed suicide. In addition, Joyce advises the school newspaper, the *Meadowlark,* which last year caused a sensation by printing a survey showing that one in every five senior girls had had at least one abortion; the issue included a blistering editorial on freedom of choice. Joyce fought her way through quite a bit of nastiness over that; there were parents who wanted her to name names, and other parents who just wanted it all hushed up (unfortunately, *Newsweek* ran a little blurb about it), and still others who wanted the editors expelled and Joyce fired.

She is still rambling on about last night and how she thinks the intimacy exercises have really developed her tactile sensations and how she can finally trust Eddie enough to send him some signals. Maybe she notices that I am staring off into space.

"When you're married," Joyce says, "I mean when you've been married as long as you guys, do you think it gets easier to communicate on a nonverbal level? My counselor says that our signals and our signal vocabularies tell a lot about our agendas."

I do not tell Joyce that my husband and I have a new joke: we refer to making love as "waking the baby." The last three times we tried, each attempt already a victory over fatigue and the lure of a dark, happy sleep, the baby has woken, loud and frantic in the next room. So last night when he muttered to me, raising his eyebrows and leering, "If we go to bed early, we might have time to *wake the baby*," of course I knew just what he meant, and we both laughed, but by the time I had taken my shower he was sound asleep, and three seconds later so was I. The baby stayed asleep till four in the morning; then she woke up, nursed, and got all playful and cute and cooed and laughed at me until almost six. I sat in the rocking chair, rocking rhythmically, trying to stay conscious. I could imagine my head falling back, my arms opening out, the baby falling to the floor, the rocker rocking on.

Eddie is making progress. This week, in the intimacy counselor's office, he officially offered to commit to a long-term serious pair-bond with Joyce. Pretty amazing, Joyce tells me, when you consider that the word *commitment* all by itself used to give him hives. Unfortunately, Joyce was unable to trust him sufficiently to accept his offer.

"What do you think, was he just jerking my chain?"

"Maybe he was pushing your buttons?" The hell with yogurt; today I am eating leftover roast pork lo mein. And I am anxious too; in my senior honors biology class this morning, a boy named Angus Moriarty had some kind of breakdown. The students were divided into two groups of six, each group dissecting a fetal pig, and Angus, who is tall and pale and sarcastic, was reading aloud the instructions to his group when he suddenly began laughing in a strange forced way. Then he put down the dissection manual, climbed onto the lab table, and made a speech. "Friends, Romans, countrymen, pigs!" he said. "Just because the jangling in the air will not stop, we can still take power! Don't listen to what they are saying, don't let the blood begin to flow!" And on and on. For a minute I thought it was a stunt gone wrong, but as he kept going, it became clear that something was much more wrong than that. With the help of Gabrielle, a very strong girl who strokes the varsity crew team, I got Angus off the table, put an arm around his stiff shoulders, and led him to the school nurse's office. Then I went back to my classroom, where we packed the pigs into their formaldehyde and listened for the siren of the ambulance. Word around the teachers' lunchroom is that Angus stopped taking his lithium (no one had known he was on lithium), or maybe took cocaine on top of his lithium.

The intimacy counselor approved of Joyce for hesitating; it meant, he said, that she was finally coming to understand that for a meaningful relationship to work, both parties have to undertake informed affirmation. "Before I can say yes to Eddie, I have to say no to him, just to give value to myself and to saying yes."

Late one night, my husband and I have the baby in bed with us. She is in what he describes as her give-me-a-lever-and-a-place-to-stand-and-I-could-eat-Chicago mode, her face covered with milk, her mouth fastened noisily to my breast. My husband is providing appropriate sound effects. "Um-yumm," he croons, smacking his lips. "Ummy-yummy, sucky sucky, never stop, oh no, slurp slurp slurp!"

"We could put her in her crib and see what happens," I suggest after half an hour.

"She might eat it." He and I are both in some not unpleasant place on the other side of exhaustion.

"I feel like this bed is a raft and I can't climb off," I say, thinking of Barbados, of myself floating on an inflated cushion on turquoise water.

"I know which one of the three of us will still be alive when we're rescued," says my husband, bringing his face close to the baby's head. She looks up from her work for one second, gives him a beautiful smile, then goes back to sucking.

Angus has been out of school now for a week. There are lots of rumors; a rather beautiful freshman girl who dresses and poses like a ballet dancer is supposed to have written him a nasty note, telling him to stop following her around. There is a story about a summer spent in an institution several years ago, all very posh and discreet. Someone says he tried to cut his wrists once, someone else that he heard voices telling him to stab the girl. I cannot bring myself to continue with the fetal pigs, which are strong stuff anyway, so I start a unit on tidepools, which I had been planning to do later on, in the spring. There is no point in going to the shore to poke around in January, but I promise the students a field trip when it gets warm.

Joyce and Eddie have realized that they are both frightened of what the intimacy counselor calls aloneness. However, they cannot make couplehood out of the absence of aloneness, the counselor has explained.

"Couplehood?" I say to my old friend Joyce, the English teacher.

She has the grace to look mildly ashamed. "Call it what you like," she says. "The real point is that it's clear to me and Eddie both that it's worth putting more energy into building this relationship, but we have to put the foundation in before we can build on it."

I am thinking wistfully about last year, when Joyce was having an affair with the twenty-two-year-old Yale graduate Pleasant Meadows had hired to teach shop. They didn't eat lunch together because they were keeping it secret, and she spent lunch hours whispering to me about his skill, his stamina — where were the twenty-two-year-olds like that when *we* were in college? The lunches used to leave me titillated and envious and amused; I would walk back to my classroom thinking that the school was a place of interest and intrigue, and not just for the students, forming cool, casual couples in the hallways as if they have accidentally found themselves together. The shop teacher is now at Stanford, in his first year of business school.

I want to talk about myself, but my only subject is fatigue. How tired I am, how my skin and my bones and my nerve cells are all tired. What I would give to sleep for eight hours straight. Or I could talk about the baby, of course, but that conversation is proscribed, ever since Joyce decided that she wants marriage and children and started using phrases like *before it's too late.* And this is a woman who was screwing around with recent college graduates last year; she's only thirty-one. I blame Eddie for all this; he's the one who said to her, after they had been together for a month, that he wanted to feel the relationship had a long-term future, but it was only fair to tell her that in the past he had had problems with intimacy. He added that he wanted to have children in time to play baseball with them, he didn't want to be just some old codger when his children were young. Baseball-playing apparently dries up even earlier than the menstrual flow. How charmed Joyce was by this! How she rushed with him, hand in hand, to the intimacy counselor!

I have not met Eddie. What with the baby and all, I have not been up for any double-couple evenings. Joyce says Eddie has a pretty good body, he works out, he keeps in shape. He has a little mustache, she says, his hair is going thin on top, he dresses well. The truth is, I don't want to meet him, I suppose.

My breasts have finally adjusted to the schedule and no

longer fill up like water balloons in the middle of the day. My first month back at work, I was teaching a class on the cell when the snaps on my nursing bra suddenly popped open as my engorged chest made a desperate bid for freedom. Bing, ping, and away we go! I could feel them bobbing around under my sweater, and I crossed my arms tightly over my chest and stood stock-still in front of the room while my voice went on explaining to the students, making them understand the difference between the plant cell and the animal cell, the significance of the cell wall, the issue of photosynthesis.

They're very good, my students. The senior honors biology class, now short one student, is probably the nicest class I have ever taught. Even before Angus went crazy, they were unusually gentle and polite with each other; I never felt that anyone was self-conscious about talking in class, even about guessing, speculating, trying to figure out an answer out loud. This is quite rare, especially among the good students, the crème de la Pleasant Meadows, as they wait out the Ivy League early decision letters. Often they seem to be under the impression that the college admissions offices have spies who have wired the classrooms for sound: Aha! he confused chloroplasts and mitochondria! Throw his application away, take someone else.

They are even gentler with each other now, and also with me. We close the door and talk about tidepools. I gave them *The Edge of the Sea* by Rachel Carson to read, and one day, to my surprise, we found ourselves talking about what would draw a person to spend her life studying the sea and the plants and animals it washes up and leaves behind. Gabrielle actually came right out and said in class that she was thinking seriously about becoming a marine biologist, and of course it was convenient, since she could major in biology in college and that would satisfy her father, the surgeon, who wants her to become a radiologist.

"Why a radiologist?" asked one of the others, Rebecca Fong, who actually does plan to go to medical school and then into genetic research. I know this because I wrote one of her letters of recommendation.

"My father thinks it's the perfect medical career for a woman," Gabrielle says, using that familiar adolescent tone of exasperation, of can-you-believe-how-dumb-this-is. "Good hours, great money, no blood and guts."

I drop off the baby at the day-care center. Her bottles go in the refrigerator, her change of clothing goes in her cubby. She herself goes on the carpet and immediately takes off, crawling at ferocious speed for her favorite busy-box. At home she never crawls like this; she knows that she has only to direct us and my husband and I will bring her what she wants. Don't ask me how she knows this, at the age of seven months, but she does. The day-care teacher says to me that I look awfully cheerful this morning.

"She slept!" I cannot keep it to myself. "She went to sleep at ten, and she didn't get up till almost six!" I have not felt so clear-headed in months.

"Long may it last," says another mother reverently, depositing little Joshua on his preferred cushion.

I get in my car and turn the radio up loud. The air seems warm enough to keep the window open, and in my imagination I am cruising, carefree. Murray in the Morning and Sweet Sue have a thousand dollars to give away to anyone who can tell them the names of any two of the Four Tops. I have no idea, but someone does, a guy named Joe who calls up almost immediately.

"So whatcha gonna do with the money, Joe?" asks Murray. "I'm just curious, you know. I wouldn't mind being in your position. Gonna blow it all on something?"

"My sister and her kids, they just got burned out of their

house," Joe says. His voice is deep and slow; he sounds as if he is digging deep into himself to answer Murray with utmost deliberation and honesty. "No insurance, nothing. This is going right to them."

"That's great," says Sweet Sue. "That's terrific. What a wonderful way to start the day! I tell you, that makes us feel just fantastic."

"Best of luck to you, Joe," says Murray. "And to your sister and her kids too, from Murray and Sue on one-oh-two."

Joyce's eyes have circles under them, clearly visible even though she is wearing more makeup than usual. On the advice of the intimacy counselor, she and Eddie made plans for a long President's Day weekend in snow-covered Maine, reserved a room in a bed-and-breakfast that combined true New England antiques in the bedroom with a Jacuzzi in the bathroom, made dinner reservations at a little restaurant that uses only local ingredients in such creative ways that it has repeatedly been featured in the *Boston Globe*, the *New York Times*, and goodness only knows where else. Joyce did not actually tell me that Eddie was supposed to propose marriage under these circumstances, but it seemed obvious that the stage was being set for a Declaration of Intent to Commit to Increased and Long-term Intimacy. But last night he told her he was getting cold feet about their level of escalating involvement and needed some time to decide whether he could commit to the commitment. In other words, he canceled the trip.

"Joyce," I say, lighthearted, clearheaded, "why do you want to get any more involved with this guy? It's just grief and more grief. He can't even go away for the weekend without making a big production out of it. What if you got married — would you want to live with someone who had emotional crises about it every two weeks?"

"I've put a lot of energy into making this relationship work."

"Joyce, are you really in love with this guy?"

"Shh!" She's right, I've gotten loud; Gruber, at the next table, is looking over with interest. "I don't know if I'm in love with him or not. The counselor says I have to be careful about labeling my emotions instead of experiencing them."

Eddie works in a very fancy real estate office in Brookline. After we finish our lunch, I convince Joyce to call up and have three extra-cheese pineapple anchovy pizzas delivered to him, which leaves her feeling somewhat better.

That night I suggest to my husband that perhaps the two of us might go away some weekend, stay in a nice bed-and-breakfast somewhere.

"Don't you mean the three of us?" he asks. The baby has just spit Beechnut strained peaches mixed with rice cereal all over his shirt, which serves him right for bouncing her immediately after feeding her.

"Well, now that she's started sleeping through . . ." I say, dabbing at him with a wet paper towel.

"Don't get your hopes up. She's slept through exactly one night. And imagine the two of us trying to keep her quiet in some hotel room."

It's true; I can picture her systematically destroying one antique after another, chewing on the spindly little chairs, throwing up on the four-poster. And in fact she wakes up three times that night, and the final time, the I'm-up-for-the-day time, is at quarter past five. My husband takes her downstairs and I go back to sleep; as he gets up, he says conversationally, "How about we send *her* away for a nice long weekend? Do you know of any reliable kennels?"

"I think she has to be housebroken," I say, diving back down into sleep as if it were warm chocolate.

*

The headmaster contacts those of us who taught Angus, and we put together assignments and handouts to send to him. We are not told the name of the "facility" in which he is staying, but every Monday his mother brings in a pile of completed schoolwork and the headmaster doles it out to be corrected. I look at his diagrams very carefully, read every word of his completed assignments, thinking that perhaps I will come across a message, a cry for help, an apology, an explanation, but there is never anything there.

I have made a firm resolution: today Joyce is going to listen to me at lunch. Today I am going to talk about myself. The intimacy counselor would be proud of me. I sit down with her, unwrap my tuna sandwich, and before biting into it, I say, "Joyce, I'm so tired I think I'm going to die. My entire marriage has turned into an ongoing fight about who gets up when, and I can't see straight I'm so exhausted."

Naturally she doesn't want to talk about being tired, and I suppose I can't really blame her. I mean, so boring. She wants to know if my marriage is really in trouble, and she asks in such a concerned counselor-approved hoping-to-hear-your-life-is-falling-apart way that it makes me set down my tuna sandwich and reassure her: no, everything is great, terrific, what a wonderful father he is, what a wonderful couple we are, tra-la. Anyway, I want to talk about me. But I have nothing to say about me except how tired I am. So instead I say, "I worry about my students. I keep thinking another one might crack all of a sudden."

"I heard that Angus mailed a poem to that freshman, you know, Anna Pavlova. A ten-page poem."

"Really? What'd she do?"

"She showed it to Daddy, and Daddy called up Angus's parents and bawled them out, and they called up the funny farm and did some more yelling, and I guess poor Angus had his mailbox privileges taken away. Maybe they put him in solitary."

Joyce has news of her own. The shop teacher from last year, the one who is in business school in California, has called her up to say he will be in Boston for a weekend and would like to see her. Should she see him, she wants to know — that is, ask him to stay at her place, with her?

This is more my kind of lunchtime conversation. Yes, yes, I tell her, and she smiles a little self-consciously and agrees. We make up a story together about how Eddie will come, repentant and eager for intimacy, to bang on her door on Saturday morning, how she will open it, slinky and desirable, wrapped in silk and lace, and there behind her will be her twenty-three-year-old stud, lounging on the couch, wearing maybe the blue plaid bathrobe that Eddie has not yet collected from her apartment, the bathrobe falling open to reveal his powerful thighs.

In fact it snows all weekend, and my husband and the baby and I don't leave the house. We stay in our pajamas and we sleep in shifts, the baby when she pleases, my husband and I taking turns. We eat some stuff from the freezer, and on Sunday we send out for pizza. Having caught up on sleep, we have a big fight Sunday afternoon about who is responsible for calling the plumber to come and fix the backing-up drain in our bathtub, which has resisted four doses of Drano. After an hour or two of pointed sulking on both sides, I go to sleep and don't wake up till nine in the evening; I then cannot fall asleep again for most of the night. I feel ready to scream with the frustration of it, of being wide awake at night while the baby is sleeping, knowing how tired I will feel in the morning. The snow falls on and on.

No school on Monday. Snow day. I stay home with the baby while my husband goes to work. By afternoon I am calling up everyone I can think of, jiggling the baby on my shoulder. Joyce is eager to talk; the shop teacher has gone off to New York for more job interviews. It was fantastic. It was amazing. He's so much fun. He's just dynamite in the sack. She's been laughing all weekend. Saturday night they drank a bottle of champagne and then went walking in the falling snow, went to the Harvard arboretum and walked all over the place in the moonlight. What a trip, up and down the hills, the trees in the snow. Then they walked all over town looking for someplace open late where they could buy food, and ended up in a hotel lounge eating water chestnuts rolled in bacon at two A.M. And then they decided on the spur of the moment to take a room in the hotel for the rest of the night.

I sit down on a kitchen chair, pull up my shirt, offer a breast to the baby. There isn't much in it; I'm dry during the day. Still, she's willing to chew on it for a while. I feel jealous of Joyce, as I haven't in months. Never mind the sex and the booze; think of just setting out into a snowstorm to walk and to play and end up wherever for the night. I feel old and domesticated, my life a cycle of responsibility, predictable and packaged up like a roll of paper towels. Tear off any day, any week, any year.

"Not only that, but Eddie actually did call," Joyce says. "He didn't come over – that would be too good to be true. But he called up to say that he wanted to see me on a strictly friendly basis – he's been thinking about his needs as a person and our needs as a couple, and he thinks we could negotiate a new agenda."

"What did you say?"

"I told him I had been thinking about my needs as a person too and I was busy satisfying them, so I didn't have time to get together."

"Are you sure you don't want to give him another chance?" I am treacherous. The baby's diaper, I suddenly realize, is full of poop. She lies cozily in my lap, sucking, half asleep.

"I cut out a coupon from a magazine," Joyce says dreamily.

"You send in two dollars and you get a catalogue of equipment for shoe fetishists. I'm gonna send it to the intimacy counselor."

The streets have been plowed, but it takes me twenty minutes to dig my car out of the drifts. Beside me as I drive, the baby gurgles and snorts and makes the purring noise in her throat that my husband calls her vibrato. I drop her off, kiss her head, turn from the doorway to see her chewing on her toes. I get into my car and drive off carefully along streets with snow piled high on either side, swamping the cars that have not yet been dug out.

"And it's another great giveaway from Murray and Sue! A trip to beautiful Aruba this time, airfare and hotel for two for five days! Have you been to Aruba, Sweet Sue?"

"No, I never have. But you never know, I might get there someday yet!"

"That's true, Sweet Sue! Hey, I'm a poet and I don't even know it."

"Okay, Murray, just reach into this magic barrel and pull out a postcard from some lucky listener. One, two, three!"

"Yes! And the trip to Aruba goes to Angus Moriarty, of West Newton! Congratulations, Angus!"

I hit the brakes, but fortunately I'm traveling slowly, and so are the cars behind me. I start up again, driving as delicately as if my back seat were full of eggs. Twenty minutes; he has twenty minutes. Will he call and win the trip? When I get to Pleasant Meadows, Angus has just five minutes left to call. I park in the teachers' lot but leave the motor running, the radio on. They are playing one of their regular morning songs and I listen carefully. "That's the sound of the men working on the chain gang . . ."

The song ends. Murray in the Morning's voice comes on: "Who's this? You're on the air! Hello, who is this calling?"

"Angus Moriarty." His voice is thick, and each syllable gets equal weight.

"And what do you have to say?"

"Murray and Sue, I listen to you, on one-oh-two!"

I turn off the radio and the motor and get out of the car. I bend over, pull out my folder full of lesson plans and graded assignments to return. I am tired, and the parking lot is hard walking, rutted with dirty ice. Still, I walk toward the school on sure and light-stepping feet. Spring will be here in a couple of months. Joyce and I will giggle together over lunch. The baby will look into my face and laugh at the end of the day. And suddenly, out of the blue, you might just win a trip to somewhere.

City Sidewalks

CLAIRE IS in a hurry, running for the bus. As usual. The day-care center asked, since it's Christmas Eve, if everyone could pick up by four today, and Claire's boss assured her that she could leave early, but then at the last minute one of his research assistants discovered that the lab would be completely out of some very important enzyme preparation by Monday and more had to be ordered at once, and now Claire doesn't think she'll make it by four. So she'll be late again to pick up her daughter, and on Christmas Eve. She hurries out of the lab building and takes the shortcut through the hospital, even though it means going through a door marked DO NOT ENTER and then racing through the lobby, where the homeless people are already gathering for the night, taking their places among the sick.

It seems to Claire that her life is made of apologies and excuses. I'm sorry, Dr. Fergus, I wish I could stay and finish typing this, but I do have to pick up my three-year-old at her day-care center. I'm sorry, Lynnette, I know I'm late to pick up Thea, but the bus didn't come. I'm sorry, Thea, I know I'm the very last mommy.

Out the automatic sliding doors and then only half a block more, and maybe if the bus comes right away she'll be on time. And Thea will be glad to see her, not woebegone and worried at being left till last, and Lynnette will smile, and everyone will wish each other Merry Christmas. Merry cold snowless New England Christmas. Claire pulls her coat closed but doesn't break stride to zip it, then glances over at the windowless graffitied wall of the hospital and suddenly does break stride, veers off course, kneels on the sidewalk. A bundle of rags, tucked right up against the wall — but she heard it cry, and though she said to herself, *Maybe a kitten,* she knows perfectly well that no kitten sounds like that. And no bundle of rags, either. Her hand is shaking slightly as she peels away first one, then another shabby blanket. Under them, securely zipped into a green snowsuit, is a baby. Red face contorted, really howling now. A baby lying on the sidewalk.

What should she do? What the hell are you supposed to do? Take the baby into the hospital lobby and hand it to someone? Call the police? She looks around, but of course there are no police in sight. They pull up frequently enough to the emergency room, bringing in people who have been hurt; this hospital, in this bad neighborhood, is widely known as the place to go if you've been shot or stabbed. How can she run into that waiting room and try to hand a baby to someone who won't understand what's going on? Then, with an unmistakable clank and a whoosh of exhaust, her bus pulls up behind her. Without really thinking about it, Claire grabs the baby up out of the blankets and runs for the bus stop. She makes it, she's on the bus, she'll be at the day-care center on time, and as she drops into an empty seat with the unexpected weight of this strange baby in her lap, she smiles down in triumph. The baby, who has evidently enjoyed the jolting run for the bus, smiles back at her, a big, adorable, gummy smile: *Well, here we are.*

All the way to the day-care center, Claire wonders what she should have done, what she should do, and rocks the baby gently on her lap. Boy or girl, she wonders, and guesses, somehow, boy; there is something about this face that is distinctly different from Thea's well-remembered baby face. Age, she guesses, somewhere around six months. What the hell kind of crazy person leaves a six-month-old baby lying out on the street in December? Though perhaps some people might wonder, What the hell kind of crazy person picks up a baby off the street and goes running for a bus? The baby looks healthy. But why not leave the baby somewhere warm, if you're going to leave the baby — but who would leave a baby?

Claire makes her way off the bus and into the day-care center. Thea is out in the hallway, sitting on the low red bench with a couple of other children and one of the teachers. "Oh!" Thea screams. "Oh! Mama, we got a new baby for Christmas?" She comes running up to grab at Claire's legs, to pull on the baby, demanding, Let me see, let me see, what kind of baby is it, where did you get it, what's its name? Everyone in the hallway is watching.

Yes, indeed, Thea has been asking for a baby. In her room at the day-care center are three children who have recently acquired younger brothers or sisters, and two more have siblings on the way. Thea asks often when she can have her own little sister or brother.

"Come on, Thea," Claire says. "Get your coat on, let's go."

Lynnette, Thea's teacher, brings over Thea's red winter coat.

Thea yells, "Lynnette, we got a baby for Christmas!"

"Thea, the baby is just visiting us," Claire says softly.

"Just for Christmas?"

"We'll see," Claire says, eager to get home and put this heavy baby down, and pick up her own beautiful, perplexed daughter, tell her some story or other, never tell her, never even hint, that someone threw a baby away, left it on the street. *I'll tell her it's my friend's baby, and my friend had to go on a trip, so I borrowed the baby for a little while — we're just helping out my friend.* A desperate need to wrap herself around Thea's perfect, strong, graham cracker–scented body, she suddenly realizes, has been building in her ever since she found the baby. "Come on," she says, as gaily as she can. "Let's take this baby back to our house!"

"Yeah!" shouts Thea, all confusion gone. "Lynnette, we're going to take this baby back to our house!"

"Merry Christmas," Lynnette says quietly to Claire, who suddenly feels a wave of grateful affection for this cheerful, energetic woman who teaches photography all morning and then works the afternoon shift at the day-care center. What a nice, kind woman Lynnette is, her long, fair hair straggling loose from her braids, her face all smiling and discreet as she helps Thea zip her coat.

"Merry Christmas, Lynnette. I hope it's a good one." And they leave the day-care center together, Claire and Thea and the strange, still amiable baby, and soon they are home. On the way, Claire starts to tell her story — *I'm helping out a friend* — and Thea doesn't even ask which friend. Instead, she wants to know, *Can the baby sleep in my bed?* The very first thing Claire does, before taking off the baby's snowsuit and looking to see if there is any identification or if the baby has been hurt in any way, or even finding out if it's a boy or a girl — before doing any of these things, she kneels and puts the baby gently on the rug in the crowded little living room, and then, still on her knees, she turns and takes Thea in her arms and kisses both cold red cheeks, kisses her tangled black curls, rubs up and down her straight little back. The scent of cold comes off Thea's body like vapor, but she is already struggling within her mother's embrace, struggling to see the baby up close, face to face.

Claire spent many years of her life thinking of herself as, well, maybe not beautiful but definitely attractive, definitely sexy, definitely someone men responded to. Tall, with long legs and a lot of curly black hair, and also, she knew perfectly well, that edge, that special kind of nerve that lets you be the first one dancing, or even the only one. She had fun in college and right after, with a succession of boys, and married Marvin, Thea's father, partly because he was so very serious, so inexperienced at having any kind of fun at all, that it touched her. He was in medical school when she married him, and he helped her find the job in the lab, working for Dr. Fergus. She actually liked working there, liked the techs and the secretaries and the young scientists much better than she had liked the people at the insurance office where she had been working.

But she and Marvin didn't do very well together, especially not when medical school was over and his internship began, and they had the same fights over and over again. That he took her for granted and used her as a convenience and paid no attention to her. That she didn't understand the pressures he was under. That he had only married her to have someone to support him financially and do his laundry. That he was tired, please leave him alone, he was exhausted. Marvin now has a girlfriend who is a doctor and presumably understands all the pressures.

But it would be wrong to leap to the conclusion that Claire is one of those wives ditched along the path to doctorhood, one of those hardworking first wives who get dumped for someone younger or classier by their newly certified husbands. There are such women around the hospital, and maybe Dr. Fergus and some other people assume that's Claire's story too, but Claire knows better. It was she who ended the marriage, she who told him, *I would rather live alone than live with you, I would rather sleep with no one than sleep with someone who is never here and doesn't notice me when he is.* Then, two weeks after he moved out, she realized she was pregnant.

In all fairness — and Claire tries to be fair — Marvin has behaved pretty well. He pays child support; he spends time with

Thea every other weekend except when he's on call. His parents, who have no other grandchild, are obviously uncomfortable with the situation, but they see Thea whenever they come to Boston, they send her funny greeting cards with checks tucked inside, and they never forget her birthday. In fact, the two biggest packages under the tree are from Grandma and Grandpa. In fact, when Claire thinks about Marvin's remarrying, as he surely will, what hurts her is the idea of Thea losing her grandparents when they turn their doting to new, less disconcerting grandchildren. Even though they will still conscientiously send birthday presents to Thea, she will have become a peripheral, odd grandchild. And Claire's own parents are dead, and her sister lives two thousand miles away and disapproves of her, of Thea, of everything.

Claire still looks fine; she's still tall and long-legged, though her hair is cut short. But surprisingly, or maybe not so surprisingly, what changed most after she had a baby was her face. Her stomach came back almost exactly as it had been, but her face is now an older woman's face, a serious face, a sometimes haggard, sometimes remarkable face, but certainly not a face full of fun. Did that happen with pregnancy, or did it happen over the first year of living alone with an infant and almost no money, up in the morning and off to the day-care center and then on to work after nights interrupted three or four times by Thea, a hungry and willful baby, dragging herself and the baby home in the evening to make supper and play on the floor till bath time? And worry: Would they be able to stay in their apartment, or would the building go condo? Would she lose her job? Would she be asked to leave the day-care center if she kept showing up late? These were her three most cosmic worries; her prayer had been *Just let me keep the apartment, the job, the day care.* For luck, she sometimes sat at her desk at work rhythmically tapping the three middle fingers of her right hand on the desk: one, two, three; apartment, job, day care. One, two, three. And she had kept them, and she still sometimes drums those three fingers quickly for luck; it is a successful magic spell, a talisman left from that first hard year.

It's so different now, coming home, Thea walking, even dancing along, taking off her own coat, eager to help make dinner, her favorite evening activity. She can mold hamburgers or meatballs, pour barbecue sauce onto chicken, even cut certain carefully selected vegetables with a butter knife. She's actually good company. After supper, when Claire sprawls on the couch exhausted, Thea bangs her tambourine and dances, entertains her tired mother with endless versions of her favorite numbers: the little-girl-named-Thea dance, the spinning-round-and-round dance, the taking-off-my-clothes dance, the wearing-Mama's-scarves dance.

But today, coming home has a weird echo of that first year and its worries. The tiredness in her shoulders from carrying the baby, a weight that you carry tightly and with great care, especially on icy sidewalks. And now the sound of the baby starting to cry. Claire goes over, kneels beside him, and takes off his snowsuit. Yes, it's a he. Under the snowsuit are faded and tattered stretch pajamas dimly printed with bunnies, and under the pajamas is a very sodden diaper.

Thank heaven, Claire realizes, they have diapers. She doesn't have to set out with two children to find a drugstore open on Christmas Eve. Thank heaven Thea isn't fully toilet trained. Actually, this has been a point of some conflict, since Thea has been perfectly toilet trained at day care for the past four months but completely unwilling to cooperate at home. She seems delighted to go fetch one of her diapers for the baby, and stands at her mother's side watching the changing process. Her diaper is of course much too big, but Claire folds down the top and tapes it to overlap around the baby's waist. While she's changing him, she looks him up and down, wondering, worrying. Maybe someone has hurt him. He could be sick, starved, neglected, bruised, battered — all the words that go with *abandoned.* But his rosy skin is without a blemish; even his bottom is pink and smooth, without diaper rash.

"What's the baby's name?" Thea suddenly wants to know.

"Tom," says Claire firmly. "His name is Tom. But if you want, while he's visiting us, you can give him another name — any name you like. Think about it."

He's a beautiful baby. Silky brown hair, big blue-green eyes, long, long lashes. This little boy is a fair, pink angel, like some Victorian Christmas card of a child.

Oh well, it's time to do something about him, time to alert the authorities. After all, she still wants to read a Christmas story to Thea and play the Rudolph tape a couple of times and help her hang a stocking. And supper. And bath time. And then, when she finally gets Thea to bed, there will still be some presents to wrap and the stocking to fill. Claire frowns — there is very little money this year, and the fact is that what she has been able to buy will undoubtedly pale beside the gifts from Marvin, from his parents. Will Thea understand that that is not because Claire doesn't love her? What nonsense, she tells herself. Last year Thea was more interested in the ribbons and wrapping paper than she was in the gifts; this year will she know the dollar value of everything under the tree?

The tree itself is small; she got it only two days ago, after Thea had asked every day for weeks. On her way to the phone, Claire switches on the blinking blue lights, thinking they might distract the baby. Dry and wide awake now, he lies on his back and looks around him, and Claire is astonished to find that this feeling too is familiar: that vague sense of triumph at having gotten the baby home safely on a cold day, the satisfaction of having changed him and settled him in a warm and comfortable room. She starts the Rudolph tape playing so that Thea will not be listening to her phone conversation, and soon Thea is watching the cartoon and loudly singing along.

So what should she do? Dial 911? *Hello, this is an emergency — an hour ago I found a baby, but I didn't have a chance to call. See, I was late to pick up my daughter, and the bus came right at that moment . . .* The baby, as if amused, brings his fist up to his mouth and smiles, as if he is pleasantly surprised to find that familiar fist here in this new room. Claire hunches over the phone in the far corner, halfway into the kitchen. Instead of calling 911, she dials the local precinct, gets switched from person to person and finally disconnected. She calls back and this time finds her way to a man who wants to know the details, and with a sense of great relief she gives him her name and address — *I'm a responsible citizen, doing my duty.* But after she finishes her explanation, he tells her that the baby needs to be reported to the precinct in which he was found, not to the precinct in which she lives. He says this kindly, not as if he is giving her the runaround but as if he is trying to save her time and trouble, and Claire finds herself encouraged by his tone to ask another question.

"What happens to him — to the baby — after I report this?"

"Well, they'll probably send out a squad car and pick him up, then they'll deliver him to the Department of Social Services, they'll call the twenty-four-hour hotline, and they'll get him settled in a foster home. That is, if there *is* any Department of Social Services left after the last round of budget cuts. We're lucky there are still a few policemen."

On the other side of the room, Thea is celebrating with Rudolph. Claire watches with her as the tape comes to an end and then starts rewinding it. Thea is now talking quietly to the baby, telling him in great detail which of her toys she will let him play with and which ones he can't play with because he is only a baby. He doesn't get to play with the Barbies, for example, or the Candyland game, or any of the special books, because he might rip them. Her voice is reasonable and friendly but firm: she's clearly doing this for his own good.

Budget cuts; they have hit the hospital hard. Budget cuts are part of the reason Claire was so scared about losing her job — still is scared.

She flips through the phone book, through the government agencies listed in the front. There's the Department of Social Services' twenty-four-hour hotline. Maybe she'll just call that first, find out what they're going to do with this baby, rather than hand him over to some policeman. She starts the Rudolph tape again and asks Thea to explain everything to the baby, crosses back to her place near the kitchen, picks up the phone again. She'd like to be sure there's a foster home waiting.

There isn't. The man who answers the phone at the Department of Social Services is named Harry Friedman, and at first he sounds tired and discouraged, a man who maybe doesn't want to listen and doesn't want to talk. But then, when Claire tells him, in a flat, quiet voice, the story of how she found the baby thrown away, he makes a shocked noise. Whatever he sees in his job has not left him invulnerable, and Claire likes him for that.

"Well," Harry Friedman says ruefully when Claire stops talking, when she asks him what happens next, "well, that's a very good question. What happens next, I'm afraid, is that we let the police know so they can try to find the kid's family, and meantime I get busy and try to find an emergency foster-home situation. The problem is, we keep a list of homes that are ready to take a kid on no notice and keep him for a couple of days, but earlier this afternoon a bad fire burned out one of our regular long-term foster homes. Terrible thing — nicest people you'd ever want to know."

"I hope no one was hurt," Claire says; she feels suddenly exposed to all the sadness and risk and loss of the city. People working Christmas Eve on the hotline, waiting for calls about bad things happening to children. Fires burning up the rooms where children have found temporary shelter. And something, whatever it is, so bad that someone left a beautiful baby on the sidewalk for her to find.

"No one was hurt," he says. "But they lost pretty much everything they had. The thing is, they had five foster kids in that house, three of them special-needs kids. Like I said, they were our regulars. So I've just been placing those kids, used up all our emergency spaces. I just got the last kid placed ten minutes ago. So now I'll start working on your baby."

Your baby. Hearing it said like that gives Claire the courage to ask the question she had no intention of asking. Thea is bringing her stuffed animals out of her bedroom one by one and arranging them in a circle around the baby. "Listen," Claire says to Harry Friedman, "since it's Christmas Eve and all . . . since you don't have any emergency places . . . what I mean is, would you even consider — I don't have to work tomorrow, of course, and the next day's Saturday — would it be possible for the baby to stay here? With me? Just over Christmas, I mean."

There's a pause; he's obviously thinking about it. Thinking about how to tell her that's out of the question; after all, he doesn't know who she is or where she lives or what she's like.

"In certain cases," he says slowly, "in special cases, the hotline supervisor does have the power to make out-of-the-ordinary decisions about emergency placements — "

"Please," Claire says, cutting him off, shocking herself. "Listen, my daughter is playing with him right now, introducing him to all her stuffed animals. Look, I don't pretend to know what could make someone throw a baby away, but don't you think after whatever he's been through, he might as well spend the holiday here, where we want him?"

"We would have to do a background check on you," he says, somewhat apologetically.

"You mean, with the police?"

"Well, I'll call the police now anyway and report the baby, let them know we're involved, and check for criminal records on any adults in your home, but what I'll personally need to do is check DSS files, make sure there have never been any problems about children in your care. I hope that would be okay with you."

"There's only me and my daughter, Thea, and you can check anything you want," Claire says, thinking suddenly of Thea's old yellow plastic baby bathtub. That's what they'll do, she and Thea — they'll give the baby a bath together, and soap all the dirt and any memory of the sidewalk away. It occurs to her to try to give herself a little more respectability, and she tells Harry Friedman that she works at the hospital, even names Dr. Fergus, tells him where Thea goes to day care.

Harry Friedman is thinking, talking slowly again in his considering half-sentences. "I don't mind telling you . . ." he says, and then pauses, as if he does in fact mind telling her. "It would certainly make things simple — I mean, finding a place on Christmas Eve when we've used up all the ones we had, and with the budget cuts and all, it's harder than ever. You're right, it seems sad for him to get squeezed in someplace where they don't really want him."

"Please," Claire says. "My little girl will think it's a Christmas present." Thea hears a word that interests her and looks around.

"Listen, what I'll need to do is send someone around later this evening to meet you, get a look at where you live. But if everything checks out — well, I don't mind telling you it might be best for everyone." Now he's talking fast, convincing himself.

"I'll be here," Claire tells him. "We aren't going anywhere."

By the time the doorbell rings two hours later, Claire and Thea have bathed the baby in Thea's old tub. They have also named him. Claire was ready for her daughter to insist on Rudolph, or maybe even Frosty, but in fact, when Claire asks if they should give the baby a new name, Thea says with certainty, "Robbie," which is the name of her best friend at day care, a three-year-old boy who seems to be completely in her thrall and follows her around all day, playing the games she chooses and obeying her orders. Presumably this is exactly the disposition she wants to see in a younger sibling or any other child who comes into her home. So Robbie it is. Claire has packed his pajamas and snowsuit away in a grocery bag and dressed him in a red velour romper that Thea's grandparents sent her two years ago; it's a little too big for him but very much in the holiday spirit. Thea, who enjoyed the bathing process as much as Robbie did and who squidged baby shampoo around on his little head with so much glee that you'd never think getting her own hair washed usually involves a screaming fit, has been allowed to button up the romper and to help towel dry that soft little head. Robbie gurgled and smiled throughout, so much so that Claire has begun to wonder whether all this care and attention is new to him, is an unexpected delight.

"Robbie might get to stay with us for Christmas," she tells Thea. "I told my friends what a great job you're doing taking care of him, and one of them might come by and say hello, but they said we might be able to keep Robbie for one more day!"

And we're so well equipped for this, Claire thinks, settling Robbie in Thea's old infant seat. Why has she saved all this equipment, all these clothes, for heaven's sake? Why this closet full of stuff, packed neatly away as if she really did plan to have another baby, just as Thea wants? But at least when Thea asks anxiously if Santa will know to bring presents for Robbie or if she'll have to share hers, Claire can promise that there will be special presents for Robbie waiting under the tree. In that closet, she thinks, are plenty of jumpsuits, certainly a rattle or two, nothing Thea will recognize or resent or want. She'll wrap them tonight when she wraps Thea's presents.

By the time the doorbell rings, Robbie is happily eating mashed banana out of Thea's plastic baby spoon, and Thea, chewing absently on a drumstick, is watching Claire feed him as if it's some kind of magic show. Every time he spits out food, Thea laughs aloud, amused but also slightly anxious; she needs to hear Claire say, each and every time, That's okay, that's just how babies eat. When the doorbell rings, Thea has just asked, "Is that why you don't want to keep him, because he's so messy?" Claire, running to get the door, hears behind that question all the anxiety of a child who sometimes senses her mother's despair at the unending mess of keeping their life moving along, maybe a child who is already old enough to wonder why her father left.

The man at the door is Harry Friedman himself, short and round with thinning brown hair combed straight back from his forehead, buttoned into a trenchcoat that's a little too tight around his middle, lugging an enormous sack. Claire makes him welcome in the kitchen, offers him tea, and then, seeing his sidelong looks at Thea's drumstick, she offers him some cheese and crackers, and he sheepishly tells her, "I wouldn't say no." *Good,* she thinks. After he's eaten her cheese and crackers, he can hardly decide she's a dangerous incompetent. In the end, she makes him a can of Thea's astronoodle beef soup as well, and Thea decides to have a small bowl herself. Claire tips the last bits out of the pan into her daughter's bowl, and as a noodle squiggles onto the table, Thea gives a shriek of victorious delight: Mama made a mess! Robbie, in response, gives a loud baby gurgle, his face covered with mashed banana, a gurgle and a smile so infectious that both adults start to laugh.

Then Claire sits down in a kitchen chair. That laughing baby – someone left him on the sidewalk. *A crack in the sidewalk,* she thinks, *he's slipping through the cracks.* Claire is shaking, maybe for the baby, maybe because these are the very fears she sometimes has for herself and Thea, slipping through the cracks, left unprotected in a cold, dark world. She covers her face with her hands and takes a deep, gasping breath. Feeling a hand on her shoulder, she looks up to see that Harry Friedman has come to stand behind her.

"What a world," she says to him, shaking her head.

He looks into her eyes, very serious. "You do what you can," he tells her. "You take care of the people you can take care of."

Thea comes wriggling onto her mother's lap, elbowing her way into a scene of adult emotion that clearly unsettles her. Claire folds up her daughter in her arms, holds her tight, while Harry sits back down and finishes his soup.

"So," he says calmly, as if everything were clear and obvious, "you'll keep this little fellow over Christmas, then Saturday we'll come around and collect him. I'll find him a good place to go, I promise."

He is tousling Thea's curly dark hair, patting Robbie on the belly. Belting his tight trenchcoat, picking up his sack. Thea, of course, wants to know what's in the sack, and Harry actually blushes as he tells her it's toys, Christmas presents for some kids he knows. "The ones who were in the f-i-r-e," he explains to Claire. "Lost all the stuff they were going to get. I just thought . . . That's where I'm going now, to drop these off."

He holds out his hand and Claire shakes it. She feels she is waiting for some other piece of information from him, some word of advice that will give the world a little more sense. He approves of her, he thinks this is a good, warm place for a lost baby; will he perhaps tell her that before he goes? He doesn't, though, just the handshake and a Merry Christmas addressed to Thea, who is eyeing his sack with intent three-year-old possessiveness, and then he is gone.

Claire sponges Robbie's face clean, wipes the banana off his fingers, carries him into the living room. The tree is still blinking, blue flashes across the worn but comfortable old couch. Claire sits down, holding Robbie on her lap. His body feels different now that he is getting sleepy; his weight sags against her a little bit, though he keeps his eyes open and fixed on the tree.

"So Robbie can stay here and sleep in my house?" Thea asks.

"Robbie can stay tomorrow, but the next day he has to go to his own house," Claire tells her. "But we're lucky, because we get to have him for Christmas." *We're lucky,* she thinks. Maybe this baby will be a little luckier too from now on. When he leaves, the day after Christmas, he'll leave with a good supply of baby clothes and a stuffed animal or two. He won't go empty-handed to whatever place his next home turns out to be. She thinks of letting go of the baby, releasing him into whatever comes next for him, and tightens her arms, acknowledging that in fact he's unlikely to be very lucky, that he will go out essentially empty-handed into a next home that will not be a real home at all. He is a cute, easy face on a terrible story. She has bathed him and dressed him and allowed herself to believe, at least for a moment, that she has fixed the world, but she knows it isn't true.

"*We're* lucky," Thea repeats. She means lucky to get to keep the baby for a day, but Claire hears something else in it too: *We're lucky, he's not.* Maybe Thea is a little relieved to hear the baby isn't staying for good; surely it has been disconcerting to see her mother paying so much attention to another child all evening. The important presents, Claire thinks, the big new toys, will all be for Thea. And that's good, right; she can't be sorry about that. You take care of the people you can take care of, the man said. And what happens to the others?

"Maybe you'll dance for us?" Claire suggests. "Robbie's getting tired. I think he's going to fall asleep soon. Could you do a dance to help him go to sleep?"

Thea gets her tambourine, holds out her arms, and gets ready to spin. "Okay," she says, smiling that on-the-edge sparkling smile. "This is the Christmas-Eve-Robbie-go-to-sleep dance." She spins and swoops, utterly confident in the blinking blue lights. She stomps in a circle, lifts up her shirt, and bangs out a rhythm with the tambourine on her plump little belly; she bends forward at the waist and shakes her head crazily so her curls whip back and forth. And all the time she is giggling with glee at her own performance, and Claire laughs too, sitting on the couch and holding the baby, holding on tight.

Exact Change

SMALL THINGS, done properly, give me a great deal of pleasure. I know what the people in the place I work would make of that, and probably do. On the other hand, I don't much care. I mean really small things. Like I commute in to work on the turnpike, and there's a forty-five-cent toll. Well, before I start my drive in or my drive home, I put one quarter and two dimes into the little clamshell ashtray on my dashboard; it fastens on with a suction cup. I bought it some years ago now at Shell Paradise near Miami. So then, driving in, it's the second lane from the right, and driving out, it's the left lane, if you want to feed right into the exact-change booth. But some people who get in the exact-change line, I swear they must be digging through their pockets right there and then; you can sit one car behind and wait while the other lines move past.

And of course, I always know there'll be forty-five cents in my purse in the afternoon and another forty-five the next morning, because every afternoon as I walk to my car I stop and buy a hot pretzel and a Diet Coke, total one dollar and five cents, and I pay with two dollar bills, and the guy at the stand knows to give me two quarters, four dimes, and a nickel. I'm a good customer. The clerical staff all have to park in the farthest lot; the close one is for doctors and some of the nurses who have been there the longest, but I don't mind, because I'd miss my pretzel. I eat it slowly, and it lasts till past the tollbooth.

You can't tell me that life is so rough that a person can't take the time to organize the little things. My life is rough too sometimes, but I've never not had the exact change. I know there's people just go ahead and throw two quarters in the bucket, never mind the extra nickel, but if I were to have to do that, it would ruin my whole day. I pull up just close enough, roll down my window, reach into my clamshell, and when that metal chewing noise begins and the light goes from red to green, it's one small thing done right to speed me on my way.

The doctors I work for would say personality disorder, borderline personality disorder, obsessive-compulsive personality disorder. That last one they would use for me. I should know, I've typed enough of their reports.

You'd think they'd be grateful, getting everything typed promptly and by someone who takes the trouble to look up words – which is more than most of them do, I can tell you. Having all the conference room schedules up to date, so there's never a conflict. And the phone messages, and the way I can always find any phone number, and even that we never run out of coffee. The coordinator they had before me, she wanted to work there because she felt at home on a psych ward, because everyone in her family had spent time on one psych ward or another, and she left the coffeepot on the burner till the bottom scorched, and never learned to use the word-processing software properly, and spent all her time telling one nurse or another about how her mother was joining AA again or how her sister had accused her of making a play for her brother-in-law. I know all this from the head nurse; *she* at least is grateful to have me instead, though I swear, the things she goes and repeats to me! Never tell any psychiatry person anything if you want it kept secret.

The shrinks, they think I'm a joke. Too careful and too concerned about details, and gets mad if someone disarranges her desk or borrows her stapler and doesn't give it back. Well, do you know what that stapler represents, Elaine? One of them actually said that to my face once. And often they like to exchange a glance when they think I am not looking. Yes, actually, that stapler represents your reports with pages attached to each other, in order. But I don't say it, not to their faces.

Other times they talk in front of me like I was a houseplant or a soft-drink machine. I hear some good stories about the patients, who are not allowed to come into the office but who come knocking on the door to beg for change so they can make phone calls, or for television privileges, or for a visit outside of visiting hours. I would say they definitely have it worse than I do; sometimes, when the doctors are exchanging a glance because I am trying to get back my scissors, I know they are thinking how much they would love to be in charge of *my* phone calls, *my* television privileges, *my* visitors.

Two new trainees started in July, when a couple of the old ones left, and I knew very quickly that one was working out and one was not. The one who was working out wore the kind of clothes I'm probably supposed to wear, earrings too big and embroidered everything and sweaters that don't fit close even though her figure is good. I'm not being jealous; so is mine — good enough. Maybe they all just think it's funny that I'm still dressing for work the way my mother taught me, nylons and a skirt and a blouse, and I save my jewelry, such as it is, for special occasions.

The new doctor who *wasn't* working out did not have a very good figure. In fact, I would call it an old-fashioned potbelly, and I was surprised to see it in someone so young. Mostly, I think, shrinks are as vain as ballet dancers and do not get fat until they are quite old. In fact, the men wear tighter sweaters than the women, all knit with complicated stitches. So the first time I saw

Harry, I thought, Well, you have a ways to go. *Body image distortion,* they write in their letters, *narcissistic personality disorder.* They are all very interested in what the patients think about their own bodies, but mostly the patients seem to be pretty sad about everything, and I would be too, in their place. And I must say that later, when I saw Harry without any clothes on, I liked the shape of him, even that belly. It looked better when it wasn't hanging over a pair of pants too tight around his middle.

This is what happened: Harry made a bad mistake, or at least that was the way Dr. Rosenberg was making it sound. Harry had ordered that this one particular patient should be on what they call one-hour checks, which means that every hour the nurse has to write down what he's doing. But it turned out that in the hour between two of the checks, the man stole some money out of Dr. Dugan's handbag, which she had left in the patient activity room, and then left the ward and went back to his own home, which sounds to me like the act of a perfectly sane person. Unfortunately, his wife didn't think so, and when he showed up she got upset, and then he did apparently threaten her with a knife, but fortunately before he did that she had a chance to call the ward, and the nurse called the police (I found the number of the proper precinct), and when the police came, it turned out the knife was made of rubber and he had bought it in a toy shop.

Anyway, Dr. Rosenberg was telling off Harry all afternoon, and right in front of me, too, which didn't really seem fair, when Dr. R. has a great big office with a couch and all. He just likes making a big production out of everything, and right near the coffeemaker is a good stage for that. Dr. R. had to tell Harry over and over that it had been a gross error of judgment to order only one-hour checks on this patient; fifteen-minute checks or continuous observation were obviously called for. Surely Harry, for all his inexperience, should have been able to see that? Yes, yes, said poor miserable Harry, tearing strips off the paper towels. I am the only one who ever puts new stacks of paper towels out by the coffee machine, and you can imagine how I feel about having the piles knocked all out of order and strips torn off the towels. Still, I mostly just felt sorry for Harry. Finally Dr. R. led him off, maybe to give him the couch treatment. I can never believe that adult human beings, people with their freedom protected by the Bill of Rights, actually pay to talk to that man. I mean, crazy people stuck in the hospital is one thing, but he has patients coming in all the time who are free to come and go; he boasts and boasts about how busy he is, how they never leave him any time to write all the books he would write. I wonder who he thinks would type them.

So when I left that day, walking toward the parking lot, and I passed Harry, and I saw how he was just standing there at the bus stop, looking off into space like a zombie, I couldn't help it. I stopped, I said hello, I offered him a bite of my hot pretzel. And I watched his eyes closely to see if it would take him a couple of seconds to place me; you'd be surprised how many of them can't recognize you away from your desk. But Harry knew who I was right away, and took a big bite out of my pretzel too. And I heard myself say, "Don't let Dr. Rosenberg get you down – he's just like that."

Harry looked surprised. Then I was afraid he was about to cry; his eyes got all glassy and he didn't seem able to say anything, so I said, "Listen, can I give you a ride home?"

In the car he told me the reason he didn't have a car anymore was his wife took it when she left him, and somehow that led to me driving him back to my house instead of to his, and there seemed to be some idea that I was going to make him a good home-cooked meal.

He also tried to tell me that Dr. R. is a genius, and started explaining some of the research he did, all more than twenty years ago, mind you, and how important it was. I didn't listen very hard; I always tune out when they start talking about their research. But I liked having him in my car; it was a cold October afternoon and getting dark too early, and the car felt warm and cheerful to me. A sentence came into my head suddenly and just hung there.

In my kitchen, watching me make spaghetti sauce, Harry said to me, "Dr. Rosenberg says I'm not working out. He says I'm out of my depth; he says we're going to have to make adjustments and find a new mode of managing things. Oh God, Elaine, I'm screwing up, and everyone knows it. I'm way behind on my dictations. I make mistakes with my patients. If that guy had killed his wife with that knife today, it would have been all my fault." And he laced both hands into his hair and let his head sink down onto his chest.

"Well, no," I said. I like the onion cut into very small square bits; I like the mushrooms sliced almost paper-thin. I keep my own knives very sharp. "It would have been his fault if he had killed her," I said. "If *you* had killed her, well, that would have been your fault." When I had onions and mushrooms cooking and the kitchen was smelling like dinner, I turned the heat down all the way and went and stood next to where he was sitting. I was in my tidy skirt down below the knee and my blouse with a ruffle and my nylons, and I hadn't spilled any food on myself. It's all a matter of taking care as you go. When he put his arm around my waist, that sentence came into my mind again, and when he stood up to hold me, I said it, very softly, into his shirt. "It gets lonely in the winter," I said.

Obviously, we kept it all a secret. I drove us in to work and let him off two blocks away. He never stopped by my desk to chat. No one seemed to notice that his shirts were properly ironed or that he was happy.

But he was — happy, I mean. I could tell. He brought me

things, and they were good things, chosen for me, I mean, and not for anyone else. He brought me a letter opener with a carved malachite handle, and it slit open envelopes perfectly, clean and smooth without any fraying. He brought me a tiny little box with a mother-of-pearl cover, the perfect size for my pair of cultured pearl earrings. To tell the truth, it surprised me how happy I was myself. I haven't mentioned my ex-husband, and there's good reason not to mention him, but the fact was that it had been two years since he had finally cleared out, leaving behind him only bad memories, insults, and anger, and in that whole two years I hadn't felt anything much for any man at all. Not attracted, not intrigued, not even irritated in an interesting way. And now, all of a sudden, here I was with a potbellied failure of a trainee shrink, and I was happy, and I had no interest in understanding why that should be.What's maybe more surprising, Harry didn't really want to analyze it either. What's more, he didn't push me to talk about my ex-husband. In fact, I wondered if that was why he was having so much trouble in his work; he respected a person's privacy, that's what it was. He could tell I didn't want to go into detail.

One thing, though, about getting mixed up with Harry like I was: I got to hear an awful lot more about what was going on with the patients. I mean, I always heard bits and pieces, and of course I typed all the dictations and the formal reports, so eventually I knew most things, but Harry would tell me the news as it happened, so to speak. So I knew about this man named Edouard right from the beginning, about how sad it was.

Edouard was a French-Canadian composer who had been married to a beautiful woman named Valerie, a harpist who had taught at a conservatory in Boston. Together they had had twin sons. When the boys were almost two, the family went on vacation to a little island off the coast of Maine, where they stayed in a simple rustic rooming house. They had the attic, which was furnished with feather beds and quilts and rocking chairs. Then one day when Edouard wanted to go fishing, Valerie decided to take the two boys to the mainland to do some shopping. Edouard was standing on the jetty, watching the little boat putter off into the distance, when it suddenly burst into flames; the motor had sparked a gasoline puddle in the bottom. He threw himself into the sea, swam as far as he could – and was eventually picked out of the water, spent and exhausted, by one of the rescue boats. Valerie had been badly burned, and Edouard never knew whether she had lived long enough to drown. Both little boys had drowned.

God, they loved the details of this story. I can't tell you how they passed them back and forth, the tragic nuggets, Dr. R. and the head nurse especially. It was nonstop with them. *Did you know he had written her a concerto, she was going to be the soloist – he says the orchestra at her school wants to perform it now in a memorial concert, but he can't stand to hear any other harpist play the part.* It was so perfect for the shrinks, what with Edouard and his wife having been so cultured and all. And Edouard had come to them for help, because his tragedy had destroyed him, left him unable to work or fix his mind on anything for long, and they would save him, help him face the memorial concert, restore him to composing, send him out, tragic and irresistible, to marry again, I suppose, and father more twins.

So sad, so sad, Harry said to me every night. So sad, so sad, so sad, I could hear them all clucking all day long. When Edouard himself came knocking at my office door one day to ask if he could store some particularly treasured cassettes in my desk drawer, I must say I didn't like his eyes. They were cold and dark as seawater, though of course with the drugs they use on the patients, you can't necessarily tell much from anyone's eyes.

Harry thought it was a big coup that Dr. R. was letting him work with Edouard. Trusting him to take care of the prize patient. But still leaning on him about his dictations, about his conference presentations. Keeping him, in fact, in a state of complete confusion.

Well, to make a long story short, Edouard was a big fat fake. Never was a composer, never married to anyone, no twins, no quilts, no exploding boat. Made the whole damn thing up, I guess for attention, though of course they had another name for it, a syndrome. He just must have liked all the sympathy and the therapy and the people trying to help him over his grief. I suppose I can understand that a little bit, that feeling I have been known to have myself, that somehow it just isn't fair that some of us have to get up early every morning and put on stockings and work an eight-hour day while other people sit around and talk about themselves and everybody tries to figure out what would help them. I mean, to me it seems like some of that energy should go into rewarding the ones of us who are leading useful lives. But then, I wouldn't trade places with the patients for all the tea in China, so I have no call talking like that, I guess.

He got too fancy, Edouard, started giving too many details. Turned out that a visiting doctor, a big-shot professor who of course got to hear all about their pet tragedy, took his vacations right in that same part of Maine. Wanted to know what island, which summer, when had this terrible accident taken place? And Edouard flubbed it, got it wrong. Hadn't ever been to Maine, and so on.

It all came out, and there was certainly a lot of egg on a lot of people's faces. Dr. Rosenberg, of course, felt that Harry should have seen it all right away. Long after Edouard had signed himself off the ward, Dr. R. was still analyzing Harry's failure to pick up the obvious clues, his lack of attunement to the subtle nuances of truth and falsehood. It all tied in very neatly with one of Dr. R.'s pet theories about what I believe he called the metaphorics of transference, but it also all fit in very neatly with his theory that Harry was just not working out. From having trusted Harry with his most important patient, he swung all the way around and started supervising Harry's every move. And from cautious, confused optimism, Harry swung around too. He didn't even want to come home with me most evenings; he wanted to go home to his own horrible apartment, where, I happened to know, he had never even moved his pillow over to the middle of the bed after his ex-wife left him. Not that I ever slept in that bed; I saw it exactly once, when we stopped to get Harry a change of clothes. I'm particular about sheets.

Normally, of course, I would say that a person who wants to go home alone should be left to go home alone and not pursued with company or comfort. But somehow I just couldn't stand the idea of Harry in that mood, in that bed, night after night. Eating doughnuts out of a box. I made up a story about how I was getting obscene phone calls, how I was afraid to be home at night. Harry came home with me and protected me, and I thanked him and told him I felt so much safer having him there, and in a certain way that was even true. I did feel safer, knowing I could fool him if I needed to and make him feel better. It meant I was a person who could take proper care of someone else, which I suppose I had begun to doubt. I made up my mind that I would take full and proper care of Harry.

Well, I must say that even before this, I had been helping Harry out with his dictations. He was a lousy dictator, with run-on sentences all over the place, never remembering the sacred format developed by Dr. R. himself. So when I typed them up, I cleaned them up. I changed the stories around so they read better, I put the diagnoses and plans into Rosenbergian format, and sometimes, if something made Harry sound like a not very good doctor, I just left it out. I mean, he had this habit of honestly explaining all his false guesses at a diagnosis, all the medicines he had tried that hadn't worked. None of the other doctors did their summaries that way, I knew for a fact, and I didn't want anyone reading through Harry's to get the idea that he was just a klutz. So I did a little judicious editing here and there, and I made sure he was all caught up.

But after the Edouard fiasco, I did something more extreme. Harry decided he had to look for a different job, since Dr. Rosenberg was so definite about the not-working-out. Unfortunately, Dr. R. was his main reference, his supervisor. And let's just say that the letter that eventually went out over Dr. R.'s illegible signature was a whole lot more positive than the letter I initially typed into my word processor. I mean, I did things like I changed "potentially passable therapist" to "potentially pathbreaking therapist." Lots of that. But I didn't forge Dr. Rosenberg's signature, even though I easily could have. I just gave him the letter, and he signed it. They don't look, and they don't listen. I would no more sign a document without reading it than I would pee on the floor.

Harry never knew what I did, but then he never knew what Dr. R.'s original letter had been like either. He got most of the jobs he applied for, and he took one in San Diego, and at the end of June he'll move away. He hasn't asked me if I'll come, and if he does, I don't think I will. He still comes home with me a couple of nights a week, and we still keep it secret, but I think when he goes, he goes. The thing is, I'm sure he chose San Diego because it's about as far from the coast of Maine as you can get and still be in this country. None of them can adjust to losing that story, I think. It's like they feel that if Edouard was lying, then what good are they?

I will stay where I am. I will keep my job. When they carry off my Scotch tape dispenser and forget to return it, I will order another from central supply. I am the only one who knows where the requisition forms are kept. And then, if I am patient and I wait, what I want will come to me.

Freedom Fighter

Jan and Marcie go away for the weekend. Two women, friends since college twenty years ago, sit in a car driving north out of Boston. One of them is so pregnant that it's her last chance to go away for a weekend; in another week, she comments to her friend, she'll be in that ninth month, that month when you aren't supposed to go too far from the hospital. "Well, you should know," her friend replies, a reference to the fact that the pregnant one is also an obstetrician, a professional giver of advice to the pregnant.

"Well, you know," Jan, the pregnant one, says honestly, "there's always a certain amount of do as I say, not as I do." The truth is, she is already slightly over that borderline; it's a tiny bit reckless to be going out of town. But this is her third baby, a third safe and boringly uneventful pregnancy (from her professional obstetric point of view). Jan's babies don't come early; she expects this one to arrive, as the other two did, in the week after the due date — and her due date, needless to say, is professionally accurate. So it's just a theoretical recklessness, really; Jan knows perfectly well that she will trundle her pregnant belly back to Boston at the end of the weekend and she and her husband, Alan, will wait out another four weeks or so.

"Your patients must look at you and think, That woman sure knows what she's talking about," says Marcie, her friend, not pregnant, not planning ever to be pregnant again. "Do as she says, do as she does, you're all in this together." *But not me, not ever again* is what her voice suggests. There they are, the two of them, like some bad movie about women's choices: Marcie who got pregnant and dropped out of college and married and divorced and lived hard and poor, Jan who plodded on through medical school and married at almost thirty and will soon have three children spaced at neat three-year intervals, while Marcie, her grownup son now off in college, is rich and successful and busy with love affairs. "I would think it would be excellent for business," Marcie says. "You're a walking billboard for your own profession."

In fact, Jan's patients all comment on it when Jan walks into the room. "Doctor, I didn't know you were expecting!" "You're going to have a baby," they say, or just, "When are you due?"

She smiles. She nods. She does their pelvic exams, leaning forward over her belly, which is the largest thing about her these days.

"So is this your first?" they ask, these clinic mothers, who mostly had their firsts before the age of twenty – and sometimes their seconds as well. Jan cannot help it, she thinks of this as their unconscious but devastating tribute to class distinctions, to the fact that she is obviously in her late thirties but without makeup, with her hair cut short and left in its natural state and color, even her clothes, these professional natural fabrics. When they look at her, these mothers see an overgrown yuppie schoolgirl, ready now for that carefully planned, long-deferred first baby.

"My third," she says, with a certain smugness. And though they smile, for the most part they lose interest there and then. *Oh,* Jan imagines them thinking with bored familiarity, *why, she's one of us after all – probably doesn't even use birth control.* But how dare they sum her up like this, when she has spent more than a decade working on a good but stressed marriage (her job, his job, the kids, all the women's magazine problems) – how dare anyone at all take Jan and Alan and their third baby for granted? The third baby; even her parents seem to have lost interest. And after all she's done for them, too – the M.D., the two perfect grandchildren. How dare they face the prospect of a third with such matter-of-fact, here-we-go-again equanimity?

It feels good to be moving, to be in motion away from her family, her children, her parents, her patients, her life. Even away from Alan, just for a little while. Jan leans back and closes her eyes and pats her pregnant belly, and thinks about how often she has imagined running away with her belly, with her baby, how often she has wanted to escape with this pregnancy out of the noisy, busy matrix of her life.

Evenings at home, Jan often sits on the couch and talks to the third. Plans their elopement. We'll run away together to someplace where the scenery is strange and the topography is as new to me as it and everything else will be to you. The Southwest, the Yukon, the Low Country. Where seldom is heard a discouraging word. And there I'll hold you in my arms and turn slowly around beneath a strange lone cactus, a towering redwood, a tree dripping Spanish moss. And there I'll sit in a rocking chair on the porch or before the crackling fire and put you to my breast. My love.

So this will have to do. A weekend with Marcie, who is not pregnant and does not plan ever to be pregnant again. Who is unmarried, whose son is in college, an almost unimaginable stage now for Jan, whose children are still young. Carry me far away, Marcie. Talk to me of things I know nothing about, and listen while I draw to your attention the wonder of my own adventure. I want to appreciate you, and I want to be appreciated. And I want a little fun before the oxytocin kicks in and the contractions start and the prolactin starts me lactating and I become once again the creature of the hormones I know so much about. A little fun – is that too much to ask?

"I wish we had a convertible," Jan and Marcie will say to each other, any number of times. What they actually have is Jan's family Volvo, nice and reliable in a crash but lumbering along emptily behind the two of them, two ladies in the front seat of a station wagon. It's Jan's car, but Marcie prefers to drive and Jan prefers to lean back and be driven, and as she is driven along, she fiddles with the radio, switching back and forth between two oldies stations, and when she happens to hit a song about cars, driving, racing, she turns up the volume and they sing along. "Little Douce Coupe," "Mustang Sally," "Oh Lord, won't you buy me . . ."

This is one of the things you can't remember from one pregnancy to the next – like the feeling of labor, Jan reflects as Marcie switches lanes abruptly, cutting off a red Jeep Cherokee. This sense of an almost full-size baby packed in there and elbowing, this peculiar intimacy, like two large adults trying to sleep together on a camp cot on a hot night. Every move this baby makes, Jan is on the receiving end – a positional wiggle, an exuberant cascade of kicks. She lies back in her seat, free to incline it without having her children yell their complaints from the back. The baby has shifted this past week, fallen slightly down and forward, and Jan has to lean backwards when she walks. Not so easy on the ice, but it's spring; the Boston winter is over, there's no more ice on the sidewalks. And even when she's not pregnant, Jan of course does not go to work in high-heeled shoes, not with those professional natural fabrics.

Secretly, in her own mind, Jan is what maybe everyone is everywhere, all the time: a rebel, an iconoclast, a strange and estranged and angry freedom fighter. *If you knew me really,* she believes, when she stops to think about it, *you would be shocked. By my true fantasies, my true preferences, my true beliefs.* I cannot quite put a name to those beliefs of hers, cannot quite explain why she feels entitled to this certainty that she is something rich and strange.

So look: she is having a third baby; her body has been overtaken, as bodies get overtaken, especially in the third trimester, with the longings and weight and movements of an alien other. It is, believe me, a wanted, planned, discussed, and deliberate pregnancy. So why does her abdomen give her this smug and yet slightly angry feeling that she is a rebel, an infiltrator, a guerrilla? Why does she think that completing the triad of the 1950s TV family (think *My Three Sons,* think either half of the Brady Bunch), is a revolutionary gesture?

Speaking of revolutionary gestures, look at her now. Not the Brady Bunch but rather Thelma and Louise, says her husband, with what seems to be genuine indulgence but could also be interpreted as deep forbearance, the forbearance of a man who does not actually think that it is fair and fifty-fifty to leave him home with two children while she takes her stomach off for a long weekend on the road with an old girlfriend. But Alan is a nice guy, and of course he recognizes, as how can he not, that she is the one shlepping the stomach for nine months, not to mention throwing up in the morning and all the rest, though, respecting his greater delicacy as the nondoctor who doesn't really want to know too many details, she hasn't mentioned the stress incontinence or the constipation. Go ahead, Alan tells her, as magnanimous as a man is when he knows that all his wife's female friends will consider him model, will reproach their own husbands with comparisons. Go ahead and take your weekend on the road.

Marcie is in from out of town, passing through Boston on her way to New York. It was her suggestion, a little hesitant, maybe a little bit of a challenge of the I-don't-imagine-you'd-be-able-to-do-this-but-it-would-sure-be-fun variety. Yes, Jan thought, it would sure be fun. And she began to fantasize about exactly this scene, her very pregnant self escaping, just for a couple of days, from all the rules and boundaries of her complicated, responsible life. Then too, of course, proving to Marcie that even pregnant with her third child, she, Jan, is still something of a free agent. Still capable of a small deviation. Once again the way two friends can polarize each other: I represent a straight-arrow career and working on your marriage and young children at home and one more on the way; you stand for a troubled romantic life, a struggle to raise a child all alone, that child now in college and your business really taking off. They entertain each other, Jan and Marcie, with stories from their lives, but they also tiptoe round; Jan does not come down too heavily with her meticulously scheduled bourgeois domesticity, Marcie does not say, Thank God it's not me, starting over with a new baby, just when I have so much else to do.

Jan and Marcie stop to do some shopping. As they drive into the Outlet Capital of New England, the rain starts to fall. Marcie picks a parking lot almost at random, and the two of them stroll together through aisles of household goods, Scandinavian ski sweaters, glossy shoes. The stores are lumped together into minimalls with no obvious connections, and they are peopled by serious shoppers, groups of women off the big tour buses, down from Canada, up from Connecticut, which sit idling in the parking lots. FULLY AIR CONDITIONED, the buses announce on this chilly spring day. RESTROOM EQUIPPED FOR YOUR CONVENIENCE. COMFORT COACHES WITH VIDEO SCREENS to take you shopping. Jan watches a woman pile up six or seven children's snowsuits and finds herself imagining the troop of children, neatly arranged stepwise, smallest to largest, waiting at home.

Guiltily, she tries to stir her own interest: a snowsuit for

Matthew, age three and a half, big enough for next winter? You'll never find it at a better price. But she cannot imagine buying it now, for a winter that seems so impossibly remote, far on the other side of a long hot summer to come, on the other side of this baby, for heaven's sake. When winter comes, she will have a six-month-old. How can this be? Anyway, surely one of Abby's old snowsuits must be around somewhere, the right size for Matthew? Matthew rampages briefly through her mind, full speed ahead. A snowsuit, Mom? Are you kidding? What about a Ninja sword? For Abby she does not even consider buying a winter coat; Abby is six and reserves the right to make all important clothing decisions for herself.

Jan sees Marcie watching her watch the woman with all the snowsuits. Is Marcie waiting for her to start in on dreary talk about Matthew's size and Abby's hand-me-downs?

"Let's hit the lingerie shop," she tells Marcie firmly.

Is there something a little comic, a little tasteless, about a hugely pregnant woman sorting through the racks of teddys and merry widows and camisoles, fingering the silk and satin? Jan accompanies Marcie into the no-frills communal dressing room firmly resolved to try nothing on. She may buy herself a cotton flannel nightgown, but then again she may not, and no trying on is needed. But there in the dressing room is a gaggle of high school girlfriends egging one another on: Try the one with the super pushup bra built in — try it in black — no, try it in red!

A male name is invoked: what Joey D. will think of that red super pushup number! All the girls scream. Marcie, slipping into a sleeveless saffron silk gown, regards them with some interest.

"Do I detect the notes of an impending ceremonial loss of virginity?" she asks Jan very quietly.

"Really?" Jan looks the group over; her professional bias, of course, not to say sampling error, but to her they all look old enough to be her patients — that is, old enough to be sexually active.

"Only one way to find out," Marcie murmurs. She slips the matching saffron robe over her gown and regards herself in a poorly lit three-way mirror. "I like a nice feather trim — tickles you while you sleep" is all she says as Jan looks at her well-exercised body with envy. Jan can barely imagine what it would be like to try on an article of clothing as a lark, to deck yourself out and admire the result. In a month she will have this baby, and then, of course, she gets to have her body back.

Marcie, in her slinky saffron silk and feathers, turns her back to the three-way mirror and faces the group of high school girls. "So, ladies," she says pleasantly, "special occasion coming up? Joey D. himself, as it might be?"

The girls stare at her, blank-faced, all giggling stopped. Marcie shrugs. "I myself have two lovers in two different cities these days," she remarks to Jan.

"Like an airline pilot," Jan offers. "Is it as much fun as it sounds?"

"You'd be good at it — you like schedules," Marcie says.

No, I don't particularly like schedules, Jan wants to say. Or rather, *Hey, there's more to me than schedules and stomach.*

The high school girls are dressed again in their own clothes, and are giggling again, shaking with suppressed laughter, barely polite enough to wait till they are out of the dressing room to start in — the outfit with the feathers! the two lovers like an airline pilot! And off they go.

Jan is hurt by the "you like schedules" and feels silly to be hurt. She checks out a crowded rack of assorted items at the back of the dressing room, holding up clothes that strike her as particularly ornate. "Can you imagine?" she asks, holding up against her something that looks like a bathing suit made entirely of black lace with emerald green ribbon garters hanging down from it.

She finds a robe, a silk kimono, crowded among velour gowns with zippers and hoods on one end of the rack. She holds the robe out to Marcie, who reaches and takes the two sleeves in her hands as if to dance with it. Midnight blue silk with flocks of gray geese flying across it; Marcie wraps the robe over her saffron ensemble. She is five foot eight, but the robe puddles on the floor at her feet. Good, she nods. "This one's a keeper." Obscurely, Jan feels forgiven.

The sales clerk is apologetic when Marcie goes to make her purchase: the robe shouldn't really be here at all. It's a man's robe, as you can see — she points to the extra inches of fabric. It was supposed to go to our other store, the one in the Bargain Barn complex. I can show you some very nice silk robes —

But Marcie pays cash. A lot of cash; even after all the discounts, the robe costs almost two hundred dollars. Marcie actually has hundred-dollar bills in her wallet; Jan looks on, impressed. For years and years Marcie lived on the edge financially. Never any child support from the brief and bad marriage that produced her son. Some really historically terrible jobs: night hallway monitor in a residential home for emotionally disturbed teenagers, proofreader of discount coupon books. Jan used to wonder about offering money, not that she had a great deal herself during those years. Finally she did offer, one difficult winter when Marcie's son had a series of ear infections and they had no health insurance, and Marcie said no but let Jan mail her sample antibiotics pilfered from the hospital supply. Jan actually felt more uncomfortable about that than she would have felt about sending a check, but she mailed off several care packages of powdered amoxicillin samples. She wonders now whether Marcie even remembers this, or whether it was just one more penny-saving exigency in a life that was nothing but scrimping and trying to get by. Certainly for years, when Marcie would call, Jan tried always to say, This is a bad time, I'm busy, can I call you back in a little while? Never actually saying, Let it be my nickel. It's kind of a trip now, watching Marcie with her bankroll, especially since she's still wearing the robe.

Marcie works as a consultant to hotel restaurants. Flies all over the country, sometimes all over the world. Stays free in any city she goes to. This is a business she sort of lucked into five years ago; to Jan, on the phone (her nickel), it sounded like yet another not-very-promising job. *Yes, sure, it'll be interesting.* And then eventually Marcie went into partnership with the guy who founded the business, and then last year he retired and she bought him out. Jan cannot help being impressed with the serendipity of it all; she herself does a job that required some pronounced early-on decision-making — set your goals and work step by step to achieve them. Marcie had no idea that hotel consulting was her destiny, and look at her now.

Indeed, look at her now. Jan sits across the table from her oldest friend as they eat hamburgers. In answer to a casual question about how her appetite has been affected by her pregnancy, Jan realizes with stricken self-consciousness that she has run on far too much. Nausea the first trimester, still some heartburn, can't tolerate cruciferous vegetables very well. Marcie looks pained, and who can blame her? Actually, what this baby likes is ice cream. Evenings, Jan allows herself a little dish, her calcium, her reward for gaining less weight this time than with either of the other two, for going to the gym right into the second trimester, until she finally gave it up with a sigh of relief that lasted for weeks. After the ice cream she leans back to give the baby more scope, and the calisthenics begin. Without benefit of exercise machines, the baby works each muscle group.

"How's Ricky?" Jan asks, determined to turn the conversation back. I talk your ears off about mine; now tell me about yours. Remember when he had the ear infections and I would mail you the drug samples?

"He's fine." Said with a certain firmness, as if period, end of sentence.

"He's still liking college?"

"College is fine."

"What's he majoring in again?"

Marcie looks her in the eye. "I don't really want to talk about him. I know he wouldn't like to think I was using his life as fodder for my friendships."

Jan, stung and more than a little bit hurt, can only nod emphatically.

Back in the car, heading north again, she thinks about why she feels so smartly put in her place. The truth is, she would like to talk – she has been waiting, she now feels, for weeks to say various things to Marcie, to take her life apart and examine it and say what she cannot say to her husband and would not say to a friend or colleague who lived nearby. To regard herself and her family with wonder and irony rather than take them for granted and assume that family life is the lot of us all, that you just have to choose between the Volvo station wagon and the minivan. Marcie might shake her head and wonder why Jan is doing this, but Jan would appreciate a little wonder, even a little shock, even a little awe. Maybe it's not *your* revolutionary gesture, but it's a revolutionary gesture nonetheless. When you make radical and sudden changes, that's revolution. Movement, tumult, change.

The baby moves tumultuously inside her, maybe reacting to the hamburger, and Jan closes her eyes.

Jan and Marcie find a place to stay. They've parked in a famously quaint fishing village, prowled the colonially cute main street, and resisted any number of "country" souvenirs, things in the shape of geese or made of gingham. In fact, they've been on a goose quest, inspired by Marcie's new flock-of-geese robe; they've been, as Marcie puts it, exploring the goose motif. Finding goose items everywhere, keeping score, investigating each and every store till one of them finds the goose. It's been a terrific afternoon; they are having a blast. In fact, they say that to each other all afternoon: what a blast. It's drizzling, but only a little. And they find a room in a bed-and-breakfast first crack out of the box, a VACANCY sign right there by the side of the road.

Maude's, the place is called. Not actually Maude's Cozy Nook or anything like that, but that's about the size of it: lace at the windows and an antique teddy bear carefully propped against an old black flatiron on a sea chest. The room has two nice white wooden beds, thick quilts.

Jan thinks about her fantasies of taking this third baby away somewhere — of course, not to someone's antique-filled bed-and-breakfast nook. Getting spit-up on the feather beds. Pushing the antique bear aside to change diapers on the chest. She looks around the room.

"No place I have ever lived has ever looked like this," she says. "Or ever will."

Marcie looks around too, less impressed. "Why would you need so much old lace and Victoriana? Maude is Maude. "

"Sometimes I wish that I could have some small arranged space in my life. Some room that looks the way it looks for *effect*. You know?"

When they go walking on the beach that night after supper, the moon is full and low. There are boulders to climb, but Jan can't climb them. Her belly is too big; she's way off balance. She sits down carefully on a rock, and Marcie goes on ahead a little, almost out of sight. Jan draws up her legs, balances deliberately. Thinks briefly of two patients who have been on her mind, reviews her children, the two at home, the one here with her, rubs her now slightly protruding umbilicus, which has been forced out of its refuge by the pressure from inside. Then starts to think of all the things she has to get done Monday. Abby's new shoes for soccer; the plumber about the longstanding leak in the downstairs bathroom so it can maybe get fixed before the new baby comes, so she can maybe discourage the older children from always using the upstairs bathroom.

"Enough!" Jan says it out loud. She belches slightly, a pregnant belch, after the indulgence of too much lobster, too much melted butter. *Here I am on a rock in the moonlight, beside the Atlantic Ocean. Let me be in this moment, just me and my belly. I am a freedom fighter, I am my secret self. Let the salt-filled wind come howling in off the wild Atlantic and sweep over me — anything is possible!* She lumbers to her feet, tilts a little, thinks for one crazy moment she's going right off the boulder. Her well-trained medical mind instantly provides an entire scenario; she lies broken and injured on the wet sand, and then — oh, melodrama — the baby starts to come!

"Need a hand?" Marcie has appeared on the next rock. She stands so well balanced, so sure of her footing. She can even extend a hand, and Jan grips it gratefully, steadying herself.

Jan calls home for the first time. As they stroll back through town, heading for Maude's, inevitably they pass a pay phone. And inevitably Jan thinks with a faint qualm of home and hearth. "Do you mind?" she asks, feeling self-conscious, feeling silly for feeling self-conscious. After all, there is no phone in their bower at Maude's.

As Jan punches in the long series of numbers necessary to call her home number and charge it to her phone card, Marcie gestures: Do you want me to walk on, give you privacy? Jan grimaces no, shakes her head; it's only Alan — who needs privacy? Yet she feels self-conscious, feels like she is playing an unenviable part, obliged to check in, can't be away for twelve hours without calling home. Some freedom fighter.

She imagines a very quick conversation about nothing: I'm on a street corner in Maine, how're you, how're the kids, we're fine, thanks for sending me off. When Alan answers he is preoccupied with some sports event he is watching on television, his own indulgence with the kids in bed and Jan away, and their conversation is indeed brief and functional. But somehow all through that quick conversation, she is most conscious of Marcie's ironic eye. As they set off for the bed-and-breakfast, Jan finds she is tensed, waiting for some patronizing remark.

"Why don't we stop at the convenience store and get cookies?" Marcie says.

"How will Maude feel if we get crumbs on the objets d'art?"

"We won't tell Maude," Marcie says. "We'll lie in our beds and eat cookies and go to sleep without brushing our teeth."

Marcie stops for a hitchhiker. They're driving north, through what is a fairly heavy rain. They lingered over brunch, packed up, moved on with somewhat deliberate aimlessness. Actually, Jan has been rather enjoying the hypnotizing back-and-forth of the windshield wipers, the persistence of the drops drumming on the pane. It's conducive to conversation; as Marcie drives them steadily on, they talk easily about the shapes of their lives. Marcie's fantasy of what she will do if she makes a lot of money in the stock market: live on a boat in the Caribbean, learn to scuba dive. Would you want to stop working, Jan asks, and Marcie says, If I had the money, I'd stop in a minute. Wouldn't you? Well, no, Jan says, or at least she isn't sure. It's all this *stuff* she's accumulated, she goes on, thinking about it as she speaks: the skill with her hands, the training of the brain. It would seem a pity to let go of it, though there's no question it would also mean letting go of a lot of stress — and she begins to tell Marcie about the dreams she has of patients with sudden disasters, about the nights she cannot sleep for thinking and agonizing over a clinical decision made earlier in the day. The Caribbean, did you say, Marcie? Sounds kind of appealing. Just the kind of conversation Jan had imagined, the kind you can have only when you step slightly outside your life.

Then Marcie swerves over onto the shoulder and a very wet young woman is getting into the back seat, stuffing a small backpack in beside her.

"Put on your seat belt," Jan says automatically; that's what she's always saying to the people in that back seat.

"Thank you, ma'am, I surely will." A southern voice, remarkably out of place after all the Yankee accents they've been hearing. Jan turns around to look more closely at this person Marcie has invited into her car. This very wet person. She's a heavyset girl, looks college age, wearing a sodden thick sweater and jeans. Trying to polish her wet glasses on the sweater and getting nowhere, just smearing the lenses. Jan hands her a tissue.

"Thank you, ma'am."

"Are you in school around here?" Marcie asks, and Jan thinks of Marcie's son, far away at college. Understands why Marcie could not pass up a wet young hitchhiker, understands who Marcie was imagining by the side of the road.

"No, ma'am, I'm not in school right now. I've been working down in Lancaster. I surely do appreciate your stopping."

"Where can we take you?" Marcie asks.

"Where are y'all going?"

It turns out she wants to get to Portland, to the bus station. She's left her au pair job and is heading home. She doesn't say why, and they don't ask. Jan suspects that Marcie is determined to see her safely on her way, but why not, Portland is in the direction they are driving anyway.

Their passenger's name is Ellie, and when they stop for coffee and get out of the car, she does a small double take as she sees clearly that Jan is pregnant. And Jan, with her professional eye, sees equally clearly that Ellie is pregnant, though much much less far along.

"I have to pee," Jan says to her. "When you're pregnant, you have to pee all the time." The girl looks startled.

The diner bathroom holds only one. Jan comes out to find Ellie waiting, pasty-faced.

Jan squeezes her pregnant self into the booth across from Marcie, and they sip their coffee.

"Are you okay with taking her into Portland?" Marcie asks, sounding actually a little apologetic.

"Sure." They look up from their heavy white diner cups and smile at each other. It's not so bad to be taking care of someone together, even for a little while.

Ellie slides in beside Marcie, and the waitress swoops down on them. They are the only people in the diner. Ellie's color is a little better, and she is staring at a tall glass case stacked with oversize cakes and pies.

"Want something to eat?" Jan asks. "Our treat." She is thinking about her patients, about people who get pregnant before they can ever plan not to get pregnant. And then about Abby, her smart, confident six-year-old back in Boston.

For Abby's sake, and for Ricky's sake, and maybe even for Ellie's own sake, they insist on treating Ellie: Order whatever you want. A slice of German chocolate cake, a slice of banana cream pie, and a large Diet Pepsi. She gobbles down the food. Her hair is almost dry now, loopy brown tendrils around her pleasant plump face. She looks very, very young — so young, in fact, that finally Jan asks her age.

Ellie looks surprised. "Nineteen next July, ma'am."

"Are your parents going to be okay about having you come home?"

Marcie looks at her in surprise: Why so nosy? What's not to be okay? But Jan does this for a living, talks to girls and young women and not-so-young women about how they feel about being pregnant, about what their parents and boyfriends and husbands will say. *Prenatal care whether you want it or not,* she thinks, watching Ellie stir the remnants of her soda around in the glass with the straw.

"They'll be surprised, that's all. They expected me to stay in this here job until the end of the summer."

"But they have a place for you? They'll . . . take you in?"

"Well, I surely hope so, ma'am."

"Have you been to a doctor?" Jan thinks angrily that probably the au pair job did not include health insurance, whatever else it may have included. Is it possible that this poor girl is running away from a home where she was molested, even raped? You do hear stories.

Ellie is looking down at the table. Her voice is very soft as she answers, "When I get home I will."

Jan can feel her desire to ask more questions. All her customary locutions come to mind: are you in a relationship with the father, is he supportive, do you have a place to take the baby home to? But she does not pursue these questions, any of them. All she says is, "I'm sure you're going to be fine. But you have to take care of yourself, you know."

Ellie begins to sniffle a little, and there are tears at the corners of her eyes. Jan opens her purse, pulls out a tissue. There in the purse she sees a brown plastic drugstore vial: her own prenatal vitamins, the last month's installment. She takes the vial out and hands it over.

"They're vitamins. They're what the doctor will give you at

that first appointment. If you take one every day, it will help you take care of yourself. Of your baby too."

Ellie is staring at her in confusion. Marcie is staring at her in confusion. Jan feels more than a little confused herself; she is hardly the type to go passing medications around casually. But Ellie looks at the bottle dubiously for a minute, then opens it and takes out a white torpedo.

Jan leans over and takes one out as well. The two of them swallow their pills in unison.

"Keep the bottle," Jan tells her. "One a day, remember."

Jan conks out. After they finally find the Portland bus station and drop Ellie off, they head north, out of the city.

"I've been there," Marcie says. "Almost nineteen, knocked up, too dumb to spell my own name."

"I hope there's someone waiting for her at the other end of that bus ride."

Marcie honks impatiently at a wavering station wagon. "I tucked a hundred dollars into the front pocket of her backpack. Just in case."

"So at least she gets home with a little money and some prenatal vitamins. She could have done worse."

The station wagon switches into the right lane, and Marcie goes zooming past. "Good Lord!" she says, almost reverently. "How ever can you do all this again?"

Jan thinks with distant affection of her busy home, puttering along without her. Folds her arms around her belly: *No, you are not to prove a point, you are not a complication; you are my little love, my treasure.*

"I've got that afternoon pregnant drowsy feeling."

"Go ahead and sleep. I like the idea of driving your pregnant self northward through the rain. Into the unknown."

Jan reaches over and clasps her friend's shoulder. "Oh, Marce, I'm so glad we did this. What a hoot."

"What a hoot," Marcie agrees. Jan is already falling asleep.

Jan and Marcie look for a hotel room. They've frittered away the rainy afternoon: a brief walk in a wet piny woods, a visit to a pottery store, afternoon tea overlooking a marina. Now Marcie has turned inland, away from the coast road, and they've agreed to settle somewhere for the night. Jan imagines another quaint little bed-and-breakfast; Marcie says maybe a regular motel this time, with a functional shower. Maude had a claw-footed tub only.

But they can't find anyplace. They must already, so quickly, have gotten away from tourist land. No bed-and-breakfast signs, no motels, no nothing. Jan suggests they backtrack, but Marcie says she would hate the feeling of retracing their steps. Instead she takes one determined turn after another, following some instinct that does not appear to be serving her very well.

"Oh well," Jan says, "we could always hit the highway and drive all the way south, be in Boston by midnight."

"Bad idea." Marcie sounds as if she means it. And of course it is a bad idea.

Jan finds herself beginning to gabble, to cover up the marked silence of not finding any hotels, not knowing precisely where they are. "You know, if it was me at home with the kids and Alan away for the weekend, I would feel obliged to stage some kind of special dinner. It's what I always do, like I'm trying to prove what a great job I can do all on my own. Alan doesn't have any of that. He'll probably bring in Chinese takeout and they'll eat right out of the containers. Unless maybe he took them out for the afternoon, if it wasn't this rainy in Boston, and then he'll just take them for burgers or something. You know? He doesn't want me to come home and exclaim over what an amazing performance he put on over the weekend, but I always seem to be trying to impress him, you know what I mean?"

"Maybe that's important to you — impressing people." Marcie's voice is flat. She turns the car sharply onto a small road leading off to the right; no turn signal, no slowing down, no nothing. Another road without any sign of hotels or restaurants.

"It would be important to me right now to find a bathroom," Jan says with as much dignity as she can muster. She is suddenly imagining her life to come, with an infant in her arms, trying to orchestrate a special dinner. The baby crying, the older children squabbling. *What have I done? Why am I here in this car in the middle of nowhere? What am I going back to?*

"A bathroom it is!" There is jubilation in Marcie's voice; a well-illuminated restaurant is coming up on the left. The Ponderosa turns out to be a heavily western-themed steakhouse, with wagon wheels hanging from the ceiling, lariats on the wall. And an excellent, well-lit, well-heated, spacious women's bathroom.

"Next time we'll have to go west," Marcie says as they tear into the dinner rolls. "Rope us a steer. Ride the range."

Jan imagines herself on a horse, her belly nestled neatly in the curve of the horse's neck. Quite a sight it would be, even if she knew how to ride.

After they eat, Marcie asks the waitress if there are any hotels in the area. The waitress asks the manager. The manager asks one of the dishwashers. There's a boardinghouse about two miles up the road where there might be a room; otherwise there's nothing till you get over near the coast.

Jan calls home again. There's a pay phone in the vestibule of the Ponderosa, and Jan calls home while Marcie is using that nice comfortable ladies' room. She finds herself wondering how she will be able to explain this weekend to Alan, who would never go away for a weekend without a goal and object. Skiing, the beach; even once, long ago, a wine-tasting weekend. Alan likes comfortable hotels and he likes getting things right. Being able to say he saw the foliage at its peak. Not bumbling around in Maine in the rain from diner to western steakhouse to heaven knows where.

"How're you, how're the kids?"

"Hi, wait a minute," he says, right off the bat, his voice hushed and troubled. She can tell he doesn't want the kids to overhear him talking. He's probably taking the phone into the kitchen, closing the door. "Something happened today that upset me a lot. I took the kids over to have brunch at the Blue Moon, and they gave us a table right in the window, and I started seeing these kids from Abby's class going by — all of them girls, all dressed up and carrying presents."

Jan thinks fast. "Clea's house!" she says, placing it on her mental map: right up the street from the restaurant.

"Yeah, exactly. It was a big party at Clea's house. I don't think Abby noticed — she was sitting with her back to the window — but I saw them go by, one after another."

"But how can Clea have a party and not invite Abby? She's been over to our house, Abby goes over there."

"She came to Abby's party!" They say it in perfect unison, over the phone to each other, but they don't laugh.

"I couldn't resist," Alan says. "After brunch I loaded the kids up in the car and I cruised around the block, and Clea's house was all decorated with balloons and streamers. And I saw that kid Jessica going by, and Rachel Sloane, and a couple of others I didn't recognize."

"But Abby didn't see anything?"

"I don't think so. But isn't she sure to hear about it in school?"

"Well, maybe not," Jan says. She is astonished by how angry she is.

"She's going to feel terrible. They were all her friends, and they were all dressed up. I couldn't help thinking it would have been a chance for her to wear that dress with the berries on it that she loves so much."

"And her shiny shoes," Jan says.

"Why would Clea not invite her? Do you think they had a fight?"

"Clea is a horrible child, and her mother is totally tedious," Jan says firmly. "If I never have to hear about acupressure and herbal healing again from that woman, I will be very relieved."

"But you don't think—you don't think Abby is somehow generally excluded? You don't think she's some kind of outsider at school?"

"No," Jan says, trying to make it true by saying it. "No, I don't think so. But I think she'd be hurt to know there was a party and she wasn't invited."

Marcie comes striding out into the vestibule, revved up and ready for the road.

"I know it's silly," Alan says, not sounding at all like he knows it's silly, "but I'm so angry at that kid I can't think about anything else. At Clea."

"She's a horrible, horrible child." Jan sees Marcie looking at her with a puzzled expression. "Remember when she used to wet her pants and we gave Abby that little talk about not making fun of her? Well, that's what she is, she's a peepee-headed little slug. And her mother is a submoron."

It takes them another ten minutes of this before they're through. Marcie has gone outside the restaurant, and Jan finds her there, waiting patiently by the life-size plastic bronco. She wants to apologize; she feels silly about the way her life at home has spilled over into their evening, silly about the way her brain is frantically turning over and over the insult to Abby, the possibility of Abby's hearing about the party on Monday and coming home dejected and disturbed, and worst of all, the possibility that in fact this is the harbinger of some general social outcast state, the end of Abby's happy childhood. The dress with the berries—Jan thinks of her daughter's pleasure in dressing up. Would it have killed Clea to include her, to give that innocent trusting girl an extra chance to wear her precious berry dress before she outgrows it?

"I'm sorry," Jan says abruptly. "I seem to be a little unbalanced right now."

"Some little fleabitten hobgoblin with poor bladder control did something mean to Abby?"

"I'd like to kill her," Jan says as they get into the car. "And her miserable mother too."

Marcie and Jan stay in a boardinghouse. It's a boardinghouse, all right, not a motel. In the summer, according to the lady in the housecoat who shows them to their room, college kids rent rooms by the week and work over by the shore; there's a special shuttle bus to take them back and forth. Now she just has a couple of people staying. The room has two iron single beds, each with a thin pillow and a brown woolen blanket. A linoleum floor. A wood veneer desk peeling at the edges. A chair with a woven seat. And a typed list of house rules on the back of the door.

They've paid her thirty dollars in advance and parked in her driveway. Jan goes out to use the bathroom, comes back to the room to find Marcie in her midnight blue silk robe, cross-legged on one of the beds.

"You give the room a certain something," Jan tells her, collapsing enormously onto her bed.

"It needs a certain something. We've come a long way from Maude's."

"Rather more Mavis than Maude," Jan says.

"There's a very profound truth in there somewhere. Let's not dig it out."

In fact, both of them are peculiarly delighted to be there. Jan lies back and lets the baby kick; Marcie comes and stands over her and feels the activity.

"Impressive," she says.

She reads aloud from the list of rules, Mavis's list. No persons of the opposite sex in rooms. One towel provided, to be changed on Friday. No noise after eleven, twelve on weekends, special arrangements to be made by anyone wishing to come in late. Please have consideration for others and leave the bathroom as you would wish to find it.

"All the possible lives there are," Jan says woozily. Students living in a boardinghouse and working at the shore. Southern girls stranded, pregnant, in Maine, taking the bus back home. Obstetricians delivering babies and having babies. Hotel consultants. Mavis and Maude. You get embedded. You embed yourself. You escape, but you don't escape. You don't want to escape.

She rubs her belly. Soon, soon. "This is my revolutionary gesture," she says.

"Yes," Marcie agrees.

Jan rolls on her side and inspects her friend, regal and beautiful, admirable and unknowable. "What's yours? Your revolutionary gesture?"

Marcie gestures widely, as if to say — indicating her robe, perhaps — the money spent carelessly out of her wallet, or perhaps more broadly, us here together, this weekend, this room. Or perhaps, more broadly yet, life is made of revolutionary gestures. All the possible lives.

Dedication

THE BABY is two weeks old, and Martin's wife is leaking. When the baby cries, her breasts start to leak, and her shirts all have dried milk stains, symmetrically placed, one on each side. At night the baby sleeps in a bassinet next to their bed and wakes up crying, and Martin in the morning finds damp patches where the milk leaked onto the sheets.

Everything is leaking. Martin's wife holds the baby to her shoulder after nursing, always murmuring the same ritual phrase. "Big burpee," she croons, drawing out "big" into two syllables for emphasis. And the baby burps, often leaking a little milky stuff, and automatically his wife murmurs, "Good girl, what a good girl." The baby leaks out the other end too, though Martin knows his wife is conscientiously trying to spare him all exposure to diapering. He suspects that she doesn't think he'll be able to take it.

Martin's wife, Julia, has always been both superbly organized and extremely neat, and he has a little trouble adjusting now to all the stains, the disorder and dampness. She showers sometimes twice a day, but a few hours later she no longer smells like herself; she smells of milk and faintly even of blood.

She is still superbly organized, in her way — look how she had the baby in the second week of summer vacation, after submitting all her grades. Look how she nurses the baby; she had a special nightgown all ready, with slits in the front, and a pile of novels she had been meaning to read. He finds her in the rocking chair, the baby sucking away for dear life and Julia reading her way through one book after another.

She marks her place with a finger, looks up at him, and smiles. He wants to say, I love coming home and finding you like this. He thinks of saying, It's still hard for me to believe, or maybe, There are times when I can't quite believe this is all real — but how can he say that to the one who is leaking, to the one who is still even bleeding, to the one with the baby clamped on to her body?

"You can take Jimmy to the chess tournament tomorrow, can't you, Martin?" Organized Julia, marking her place, checking on her arrangements.

"Yes, of course," he says. "I told you I could." Having in fact forgotten all about the chess tournament. Having in fact made an appointment to have coffee tomorrow morning with an old friend, out of touch teaching in Italy for a couple of years, who expressed perhaps overdone surprise at learning that Martin was married and the father of a two-week-old girl.

So he'll move Nicholas from midmorning coffee to early-morning coffee. Part of him can't wait to see Nicholas's face when he shows up with a stepson — he didn't mention a stepson.

Jimmy, who is ten, has started calling his mother the Mammal. He seems to be mildly amused and mildly disgusted by the whole baby business, and with Martin he affects a male camaraderie, which Martin is glad to reciprocate. Tomorrow morning, Martin plans, he will ask Jimmy if he wants his coffee black, and Jimmy will grin.

In fact, the next morning Jimmy goes to collect all the drinks, the two coffees for the men and his own hot chocolate, and

Martin takes advantage of his going to use a line he has used before, trying to get Nicholas to wipe that comically flummoxed expression off his face. "In some ways, this may be the ideal way to have children," Martin says. "When I married Jimmy's mother, I essentially acquired a very bright child at the age of seven. I just skipped all the early stuff, all the years before he could talk. Instead, we had the opportunity to befriend each other. To form a relationship based on mutual regard."

For the first time, this well-worn line seems to Martin both pompous and specious. At home, he imagines, Julia is curled up on the couch holding the baby. The baby, newly awake, opens her eyes wide and reaches out with her hands, reaches out for nothing. "Froggy," Julia will say softly, or maybe "Fishie." And kiss the baby on her cold little nose, and smooth down the tracing of dark hair on her head. And here is Jimmy, careful and important, back with the drinks and the croissants. In fact, Martin is very proud of being close to Jimmy; it is just the kind of thing so many of his friends thought he would never be able to do. Look at old Nicholas, fussy and affected and disbelieving, taking his coffee now from Jimmy, sipping it with the elaborate disdain of one who is accustomed to *Italian* coffee.

"Jimmy's playing in a chess tournament today," Martin says. "I'm taking him. I'm looking forward to watching him play."

"I probably won't do very well," Jimmy says nervously. "A lot of the kids will probably be better than me."

Nicholas coughs. "I can't quite imagine chess as a spectator sport," he says, without looking directly at Jimmy.

"He beats me every time," says Martin. And thinks with some pride that he will happily spend the day watching a game he doesn't like.

At home, the baby will look around a little more, now folding her hands in front of her, and then begin turning her head to the side, insistently, mouth open. By then Julia will be leaking. The baby is the most beautiful thing Martin has ever seen.

Nicholas does not actually ask, How did this happen? Does not actually say, My God, will wonders never cease, old Martin married and the father of two. What are we coming to? And Martin does not feel pressed to explain or to tell this new and more varied story of his life. During the first year of his marriage, he told it again and again, developing lines like that silly remark about Jimmy and the ideal way to have children. He understood that his friends did not expect him to get married, not in his late forties, all of a sudden. Some of them probably assumed he was gay, which was not true and never had been, while others, like Nicholas, for example, had known one or another of the quiet, serious, literary women with whom he had had quiet and ultimately insignificant love affairs. He can see his old life, he thinks, through Nicholas's eyes, Nicholas who also wanted to be a writer but never published a line and now lives this somewhat itinerant English-teaching life. To Nicholas, Martin has always had it easy, his love affairs controlled, his books published and reviewed.

"She's a biologist" is all he says now. "My wife — Jimmy's mother."

"A molecular biologist," says Jimmy.

Jimmy's father is a biologist as well, but he does not mention that. Julia divorced the guy five years before Martin met her. Jimmy has no clear memory of this man, who moved to Washington, D.C., to work at the National Institutes of Health (which Martin now knows is plural) and gradually stopped paying child support. No one has heard from him in years. Martin thinks of Julia, at home with the baby, of Julia ten years ago, at home with baby Jimmy. What a creep, he wants to say to

Jimmy, but after all, does Jimmy really want to hear that? I'll never disappear on you, he wants to say to Julia; tonight, at home, in private. Where Jimmy can't hear.

Jimmy knocks his cup over, and the little bit of hot chocolate left in the bottom trickles onto the table, causing Nicholas to pull back with too much dramatic horror. Oh, come off it, Martin wants to say. He's nervous about the chess tournament. He's not normally a clumsy kid. Martin blots up the chocolate, smiles at Jimmy, who doesn't smile back.

"I'm probably going to lose," Jimmy says dully.

"Here," Martin says, handing him a couple of bucks. "Get another drink."

"You don't have to do that just because I spilled it," Jimmy says. "It's okay."

"A fellow needs plenty of hot chocolate on board before he plays championship chess," Martin tells him. "Get another cup. If you don't want it all, pour some into the dregs of my coffee, and we'll call it a mocha latte. New house specialty." And Jimmy goes off obediently to the counter.

Martin sees Nicholas looking at him, quizzical and ironic, and launches into the speech he wasn't going to give.

"I was writing one of my mysteries," he says, and Nicholas's expression becomes even more ironic. Nicholas, of course, only recognizes Martin's "serious" novels, short and carefully dense stories about complicated unhappy people. Each one takes him a long time to write, and he suffers over them in a recognizable literary way. And each one seems to Martin himself extremely incendiary; he has felt for years that he is always stealing plots from the lives of people around him, from his friends' marriages and divorces, their emotional convulsions, their failures and their collapses. But the critics, when they complain, complain that his novels are too much alike, too clearly reflective of his own inner landscape. Still, he gets taken seriously, he gets published and attacked and defended and discussed. But for a decade now, Martin has also been writing a series of murder mysteries, intricate puzzles set in an invented college town, solved by a mild-mannered, eccentric, aging graduate student. In every book, the perpetual student puts aside his dissertation to find the murderer and finally comes back to it in the end, the mystery solved. These books have been quite successful – all the more reason for Nicholas to curl his lip when they are mentioned.

"I was writing one of my mysteries," Martin says again. "You know, they've been doing very well. There's even talk of a TV movie." Carefully, he does not study Nicholas's reaction. "I wrote myself into a box – I had a guy who was all set up to be falsely accused. The whole thing hinged on a faked bloodstain, and I didn't know what was scientifically possible, what they could test in a lab."

The biology department had referred him to Julia, whose work did indeed involve genes and blood cells. She couldn't really answer the question, but they had fun with it on the phone, and he ended up telling her quite a bit of his plot. It was she who invited him to meet her for coffee, but it was he, actually, who proposed, six months later. Nicholas might be surprised to know that; Martin's friends have generally tended to assume that Julia willed, planned, and managed the whole romance. On the contrary, he was the one who argued her into marriage, insisting that the three of them, he and she and Jimmy, would work as a family. It was she, however, who brought up the idea of having a baby two years later and argued him into it.

"Is it okay if I study?" Jimmy has produced his battered copy of *One Hundred Openings in Chess* and already has it open, his shoulders hunched. He looks so young and scared that Martin can hardly stand it.

"Does one really *need* a hundred openings?" asks Nicholas.

Martin can see, although not understand, the squares and symbols on the page that Jimmy is studying. He doesn't think about the baby, about Julia at home, or even about Nicholas, though he knows he owes Nicholas some respectful questions about life as an expatriate intellectual. Instead he looks at his watch. Smiles at Nicholas, the busy Julia-like smile of someone with places to go and appointments to keep. "Come on, Jimmy," he says. "We want to get there good and early. Scope the place. Check out the trophies."

"Good luck," says Nicholas. "You know, I'm going to Athens in the spring. They have rather lovely carved chess sets, I seem to recall — perhaps I could send you one? A combination gift for you and your new little sister — if you'll teach her to play someday, that is."

"Of course I will," says Jimmy. "I'm the only one in the family who even knows the rules. That'd be great — thanks!" Then, more shyly, "Thank you, sir."

Nicholas's eyebrow goes up, ironic but gratified, and Martin, grateful for the thought and hoping the chess set will truly materialize, shakes his friend's hand with great warmth and great energy. It's been too long. We'll have to stay in touch.

"If I win," says Jimmy suddenly, "could you not tell Mom? I mean, don't call her up and tell her. Let me be the one. Okay?"

Martin sits in a folding chair on the side of the high school cafeteria. Jimmy is playing his first opponent at one of the long tables, and Martin watches with admiration how he concentrates, how he scowls down at the board while the clock is ticking. He does not look nervous or woeful now. Occasionally he moves a piece, or his opponent moves a piece. Spectator chess is easily as boring as Martin could have imagined, as boring as Nicholas suggested, but it is good to see Jimmy over his anxiousness and fully engaged. And Martin, too polite to read, can let his mind range back to its one true subject.

Martin is amazed at the ferocity of the baby, less than eight pounds of pure will. *I want, I want, I want.* If Julia cannot immediately pick her up and feed her, her crying intensifies, her tiny face turns dark red, and she screams so hard she loses her breath, exhausts herself by forgetting to breathe in between wails. Then there is a pause in the screaming while she gives up and takes the breath she needs, and then, louder than ever, she starts again. She does not "cry herself to sleep," a phrase Martin is sure he has heard somewhere. Julia finally lifts her up from her bassinet and the baby stops screaming and roots around in the air, making her kissing-fish face, expecting a nipple in her mouth. "It's coming, it's coming," Julia tells her, laughing, moving to the rocking chair, settling down, unbuttoning her shirt. When Julia actually puts the baby up against her bare breast, the baby makes no noise at all. Her whole tiny body shivers with determination and she jerks her head more and more insistently to the side, trying to connect with the nipple.

"The term that comes to mind," Martin has said more than once, "is 'heat-seaking missile.' "

"Relax," Julia tells the baby, guiding the breast to the proper angle. "Relax, no one's going to take it away from you." The little pink mouth suddenly lunges, clamps, pulls in on Julia's breast, and the baby's body stops trembling, all at once, as Julia's body seems to shudder in return. The connection is made; the rocking chair begins to creak.

Martin can hardly believe that he is partially responsible for the creation of anything so determined, so fierce. He had expected to be frightened by the baby's vulnerability, to be afraid of hurting it or doing something wrong. Instead he frequently finds himself quailing before the furious red gnome face, apologetic because he does not have what she wants.

You didn't tell me you wanted another child, he had said, rather accusingly, to Julia. Is that why you married me, then? No, she had replied, I married you because I love you, and in fact I love you so much that now I want to have a baby with you.

Her voice was perfectly serious. He has at times wondered whether it is because she is a scientist that she can talk in such bald and unapologetic ways.

Don't worry, she said. I'll take care of the whole thing. I know you weren't bargaining for a child. You'll end up being glad we did it.

His friends mostly shook their heads. Poor old Martin, domesticated at last. Lots of unfunny jokes about late-night noise and dirty diapers. About what would happen to his quiet life. To his writing. It's easy to imagine Nicholas making all those same jokes. His friends, Martin knows, were much too used to him. He had let them believe in him too absolutely; he had given them decades of constancy – the fastidious, soft-spoken bachelor, writing his books and listening to his records. He had a domesticity all his own, with no squalor in it; friends came for dinner to drink excellent wine and eat his imaginative salads, his veal stew, his roast chicken.

Now he suspects, watching Julia with the baby, that she had been yearning for a new baby for years and years. She seems to have ready a whole range of voice tones he has never heard, all far from the good-humored manner she uses with Jimmy, who would not, of course, tolerate being kissed or hugged. In fact, just yesterday Jimmy and Martin exchanged a smile and a shrug, listening to Julia, who was leaning back in the armchair, propping the baby up in a sitting position on her lap, face to face. "Let's see a little smile," Julia was crooning. "Was that a smile? Did you think of something funny? Let's have a smile for Mommy."

"Actually," said Jimmy, "I read in your book that they don't smile for weeks and weeks."

"Books don't know everything, do they, little Fishietoes?" Julia was kissing the baby's tiny toes, taking them between her lips and making smacking noises. "Let's see how *you* like being nibbled on," she murmured.

Jimmy looked at Martin and shrugged again. "The Mammal has gone a little soft in the head," he said, not unkindly.

Jimmy wins his first chess game. The second game will not start till the afternoon, so Martin takes him for lunch, skipping the fast-food joint and taking him instead to a nearby steakhouse, with red plush seats and lots of gilding, light fixtures, woodwork. It isn't at all Martin's kind of place, but it's obviously fancy, and Jimmy is impressed. Martin urges him to go ahead and order the sixteen-ounce New York sizzling strip steak; he himself was planning to have only a Caesar salad but changes his mind at the last minute and orders a sirloin steak and a baked potato. Jimmy is trying hard to explain how chess ratings are calculated; he has no rating yet, but a few more tournaments and he will have a number. The ratings are based on what seems to Martin complex arithmetic, and arithmetic interests him less than chess, but Jimmy does not require him to respond. Martin cuts small pieces off his steak, which is excellent, and lets Jimmy talk, vigorous with the triumph of the morning.

Jimmy's face, over his plate, is unexpectedly like Julia's. Martin has not been able to see any resemblance between the baby and Julia or the baby and himself. The baby looks like the baby. But Jimmy suddenly looks just like Julia, a smaller, softer version of her square, faintly freckled face, her straight dark hair, her intelligent, widely spaced eyes. Julia wears contact lenses normally, though since the baby's birth she has been wearing her big tortoiseshell-rimmed glasses. Jimmy also wears glasses, with round lenses and electric blue frames; maybe that's why Martin is so struck now by the resemblance. Jimmy's frames are intended to be funky, playful, maybe even trendy, so he won't look like a too-serious, too-bookish little nerd. Martin himself has perfect eyesight, and wonders suddenly whether the baby will grow up to need glasses. But he shies away from this thought, as he does from any thought that forces him to consider the baby grown up, a daughter, a girl, a young woman.

Jimmy's speech is now climbing toward the heights: grand master ratings, international grand masters, world champions. His steak is cooling, only half eaten. Martin allows himself — a much easier fantasy — to imagine Jimmy growing older, Jimmy winning a big chess tournament, exchanging a quick secret smile with Martin and Julia as he goes up to the platform to claim his trophy.

Perhaps, Martin thinks, he will dedicate his next book to Jimmy, one of the mysteries. Jimmy is old enough to read it, old enough to appreciate the dedication. But how would the dedication run —"for my stepson"? Or just "for Jimmy"? It would be a good thing to do, he thinks, since eventually he will want to dedicate a book "for my daughter," and it would be terrible if that made Jimmy feel bad.

"Do you want any dessert?" Martin asks.

"No, I don't think I should. You see, I get a little nervous right before I have to play, and it's better for me not to eat too much."

"Don't worry about finishing the steak," Martin says. "Sixteen ounces is too much for anyone."

Julia tells him what the baby wants. "I think she's just very tired," Julia says when the baby is screaming and waving her arms around wildly. "She's worn herself out and she doesn't have enough brains to go to sleep." Then she turns to the baby. "Dope," she says fondly. "Little dumbhead. We're going to wrap you up and rock you till you drop." Then she puts the baby on a light cotton blanket and wraps her tight as a sausage. This neat package of howling baby Julia puts on her shoulder, and she settles once again in the rocker, back and forth, back and forth. "You don't have to sit here and listen to this," she tells Martin. "You can retreat to your study till she conks out."

But Martin stays in the armchair, watching the rocker tip forward and backward, listening without surprise as the baby calms down, gulps, hiccoughs, and then falls silent.

"She likes being wrapped up tight," Julia says. "It reminds her of being inside. Makes her feel secure."

Julia is such a neat person that the graduate students in her lab complain about it; they are not allowed to leave anything lying around. Stray journal articles have to go in the filing cabinet, glassware goes back in the cabinets. Jars must be lined up, labels facing out; Julia cannot concentrate if something in the lab is out of place. The house that she and Martin bought together, soon after their marriage, has lots of closets, lots of built-in bookshelves. Julia has always kept it orderly, by force of personality.

Now almost every room in the house is strewn with baby equipment. There is the room that is going to belong to the baby, which is of course fully furnished; Julia had it done by her seventh month. But the baby hasn't been in there much. So in their bedroom, his and Julia's, there is the bassinet and a diapering table and diapers, T-shirts and sleepers, all piled up. In the living room is a baby seat with a curved bottom, which is meant to rock the baby to sleep, but the baby doesn't like it. Also sundry baby presents brought by droppers-by or mailed by out-of-state relatives. Martin's mother, who is seventy-eight and who had given up hope of grandchildren, has so far sent a snowsuit, two party dresses, a pair of fuzzy bunny-rabbit pajamas, and a teddy bear twice the size of the baby with a music box in it. Pull the string and you get "Au Clair de la Lune."

Not in Martin's study, of course. His study is sacrosanct. It's a beautiful room, too, a room Julia insisted on his taking when they moved in. He would have given it to Jimmy for a bedroom, but Julia said no, Jimmy would be fine in the little room on the third floor, with its sloping roof. Martin had to take the big room with the four windows, because Martin would be writing in his study every day. And much to his surprise, he is. This must be, again, the influence of Julia. It would be Julia's way of thinking, of course; if you want to write a book, then go every day to your study for *x* number of hours and write until you have a book. And that is what Martin finds he now does; no more agonizing, no more wasting hours and hours of time brewing pots of coffee and doing the crossword puzzle.

Since his marriage, he has finished a "serious" novel and is now working on a new mystery, the one he thinks he might dedicate to Jimmy. The "serious" novel, when it is published, will probably disappoint some of his friends; there is nothing in it, as far as Martin can tell, about his marriage, the changes in his life. At the same time, he cannot help thinking that his book is something new, something that has never existed before on earth. What he really imagines is people reading it and finding themselves shaken, maybe even in tears. What, after all, could be sadder than what happens in his book, that people of good will should misunderstand each other and hurt each other and lose each other?

Nicholas asked him this morning, in ironic tones, if Martin was going to write about having a baby. This is not the first time he has been asked, and it surprises him; he has never gotten such questions before. Did nothing ever happen to him that anyone thought was worth writing about? Anyway, he privately doubts he will ever write about the baby. It would be Julia's story to tell, really. He cannot imagine what she felt, having the baby inside, or feeling it coming out, or now, when that voracious little mouth latches on to her nipple.

Jimmy's afternoon opponent at the chess tournament must be fourteen, which is the upper age limit for Jimmy's division. He is as tall as Martin, and pudgy, an overgrown boy the size of a man. On his face, as badges of his adolescence, he has several bright red pimples and a faint ghost of a mustache. *He looks nasty,* Martin thinks with some alarm, watching Jimmy march up to him. *They shouldn't let a boy Jimmy's age play someone like this,* he thinks, then tells himself that size doesn't matter in chess. And after all, if Jimmy loses, he'll be able to comfort himself that he lost to someone older.

"Hi there, Junior," says Jimmy's opponent. "Ever played in a tournament before?"

"Yes," says Jimmy. "I have."

"So you know how the clock works, right, kid?"

Martin recognizes that the older boy is trying to rattle Jimmy, to psych him out, as Jimmy would put it. Martin would like to grab this big, ugly boy by the collar and warn him, "Shut up and play. No funny business."

"Feeling nervous, huh, Junior?" asks the older boy. Jimmy does indeed look nervous. He is fingering something on a chain around his neck, something that had been hidden under his T-shirt. "Is that your lucky charm?" his opponent asks.

Jimmy smiles, an open lovely smile on that face which looks so much like Julia's. "Yes," he says. "As a matter of fact, it is."

"Always wear it when you play?" The sneer is unmistakable.

"As a matter of fact, I do." Jimmy adjusts his glasses. "It's a piece of ossified whale testicle. My mother got it for me." He looks at the clock on the wall. "Do you want to start?" he asks.

⋆

The baby is the most beautiful thing Martin has ever seen. Julia thinks so too, he knows, but she takes it for granted. Of course the baby is beautiful, of course she loves the baby. Martin sits in the high school cafeteria, which is not beautiful. *Of course the baby is beautiful, of course I love the baby.* He looks over at Jimmy, who has made a move and now hits the clock to start it ticking for the other player; he thinks again of Jimmy's smile and suddenly feels himself awash in something so strong and simple that he has to blink. He thinks of all the moments of the last two weeks, of a moment a few nights ago when he held the baby at arm's length so that her face was a couple of feet from his own. She stared at his nose, and then her eyes crossed, those steely baby eyes. The baby turned her head to the side and tried to suck on Martin's hand, and he settled her against his chest and offered her a finger. Her mouth clamped on, and he could feel the suction massaging the last little joint of his finger. If there had been milk in that finger, the baby would have gotten it out. If his nail were not fastened on tight, she would have had that too.

Jimmy passed through the room and saw him with the baby. "Where's the Mammal?"

"Your mother is taking a shower."

Jimmy came over and stared into the baby's face. "She looks like you," he said, finally.

Had Martin imagined it, or was Jimmy's tone a little grudging, a little resentful? He tried, unsuccessfully, to make a joke of it. "Do *I* have a round little red face? Am *I* bald and toothless?"

"She has the same chin that you do, and the same cheekbones," said Jimmy, unamused. He left the room, kicking a perfectly clean paper diaper out of his way.

Martin would like to go and call Julia. He feels strange, to tell the truth, being away from her and the baby for so long. He would like to check in — but if he checked in, Julia would ask how Jimmy is doing, how the chess tournament is going, and Martin has sworn not to tell. He stretches, shifts in the uncomfortable chair. Everything is leaking. And he sits in his folding chair and laughs softly, amazed, a man whose friends are surprised that he is married, surprised himself by this new leaky universe. Of course. Beautiful.

"You with the little one or the big one?" It's another parental type, a big man with a big stomach and a big mustache, wandering around the room while his own son gets mopped up in the endgame at a table across the way.

"With Jimmy," Martin points. He will not refer to Jimmy as "the little one."

"These things just kill me," says the big man. "The things you find yourself doing, you know what I mean?"

"Yup," Martin says.

"I could really use a drink right around now."

"I know what you mean," Martin says courteously.

"Give me midget league soccer any day of the week," says the other man, and he lumbers off to collect his son.

I can do this, Martin thinks. In his mind, he goes on to make a speech: *Oh, come off it with this eternal-wisdom-of-women stuff. I can guess why she's crying. And stop protecting me so much. You don't have to run to save me when you hear that little grinding in her stomach. I know what it means and I could cope.* But is he making this speech to Julia, or is he making it to some larger audience — all his old friends, maybe? *Hi there, Nicholas, want to watch me change a diaper?*

Late one night, hearing the baby's cries from the bassinet, he waited until Julia had pulled her into their bed, then rolled to face them. Julia lay on her side, her nightgown unbuttoned. The baby was a small shape in the glow of the nightlight, fastened to Julia's breast. In the quiet night, the baby's slurping noises were clear and distinct. On Julia's face, Martin caught that look of bemused, enslaved adoration which he knew was on his own whenever he held the baby.

"I'm sorry she woke you," Julia whispered, protecting him again.

"I'm not." He put up his hand and covered the baby's head.

"She's so little." Julia was still whispering, though in fact a screaming banshee would not have deterred the baby from the business at hand. "Look how little her head is — it fits right in your hand."

"She's perfect," said Martin.

"We'll take good care of her, won't we?"

"Of course we will," he said.

Jimmy puts his hand up to his neck at frequent intervals to touch his lucky piece. His moves take longer on the ticking clock than the moves he made in his morning game. To Martin, it looks like all the pieces, white and black, are clumped together in the middle of the board. He cannot tell which player has the advantage. Jimmy's sneakered feet are anchored to the legs of his chair. The big boy jiggles in his seat, reaches up to finger his mustache shadow. Martin cannot believe that Jimmy can beat him, but he tries as hard as he can to will Jimmy's victory. *Make a mistake, make a mistake,* he thinks over and over, staring at Pimple-Face.

Martin doesn't know whether there actually was a decisive mistake. But he lets his mind wander, and when he comes back to concentrate on the chessboard, he senses that Jimmy is ahead. The game goes more and more slowly. Finally the big boy resigns, looking angry, and without another word to Jimmy goes stomping off.

Jimmy stands up. He looks suddenly very small and very young, standing there in his blue glasses, his sneakers and jeans and T-shirt. Martin finds himself stepping up to the boy, enfolding him in a victory hug, though this is not something he would normally do, hug Jimmy, especially in public. Not something Jimmy would normally permit.

Jimmy grins at him. Jimmy is flying high. He whispers into Martin's ear, "He tried to psych me out, but I beat him anyway!"

There are big wet milk stains on the front of Julia's blouse, another wet place on her shoulder. And there is a suspicious dark patch on one leg of the baby's terrycloth sleeper, but she is sound asleep in Julia's arms and there is no point waking her up. Martin and Jimmy come charging into the living room.

"I won!" Jimmy shouts. "Hey, Mom, I won!"

"You should see the big jerk he beat this afternoon," Martin says. "You should have seen Jimmy wipe the floor with him."

"I beat him, Mom, I beat this guy who must've been almost fifteen! And Martin's gonna take me back tomorrow for the next round!"

Julia folds the baby closer to her, reaches out with her other arm to hug Jimmy, who allows a quick congratulatory kiss on the forehead, then pulls away. So instead Julia puts her arm around Martin, pulling him down next to her on the couch, smiling at him, not with the eternal wisdom of women but as if she is glad to see him, glad to have him home.

The Trouble with Sophie

Mrs. Peterson's kindergarten class is holding a strawberry breakfast for the mommies and daddies, and attendance is very close to one hundred percent. Of course, many of the mommies and daddies will be late to work, but Dabney is the kind of school where most of the parents, hardworking and driven though they may be, can go late to work if they want. In their workday suits, their silk scarves, their tasteful ties, they can demonstrate their parental affection by wedging themselves into teeny plastic chairs and allowing their offspring to bring them paper plates of not very good late-summer strawberries. And, thinks Hannah, who with her nondescript sweater and khaki skirt is the least dressed-up mother in the room, they can congratulate themselves: what a perfect room, what a perfect school.

Across the table are two daddies with video cameras: instead of eating their strawberries, they are making movies of them.

"I just love your rain forest," says a very well-groomed mommy to Mrs. Peterson, who is moving gracefully around the kindergarten room, her kingdom. She is a small woman, full of disciplined energy, like an Olympic gymnast.

"Did Elias tell you that he helped make the trailing vines?" Mrs. Peterson says. "He did a really wonderful job!" Elias's mother smiles proudly at her son, who leads her back to the rain forest corner to admire once again the trailing vines.

Hannah is not comfortable in her seat and, to tell the truth, is not really comfortable in this kindergarten room. She loves her daughter, Sophie, and is proud and happy that Sophie comes every morning to this warm, lovely room with the marionette theater and the rain forest corner and the shelves of gorgeously illustrated children's books. Yes, this is the right place for Sophie, but the wrong place for her mother. Hannah is keenly aware of what it means for her to be late to work today: a seminar of ten students delayed half an hour. She should be in that small drab room with other people who are interested in fruit flies and their chromosomes. She is not generally at ease with small children, not in fact generally much at ease with people, period. A research scientist down to her toes, she doesn't like conversation unless it conveys information. As a matter of fact, Sophie's conversation usually does exactly that; one-on-one with her daughter, Hannah is fine. But here in this bubbling crowd of strawberry-eating parents, Hannah feels awkward and very distinctly, and guiltily, bored.

One of the videotaping daddies puts down his camera and smiles a cheerful shark's smile at Hannah. "You have to hand it to them here at Dabney," he says. "We looked at a lot of schools, but there wasn't any real attempt to nurture the child's creativity, not the way there is here."

With great relief, Hannah sees her husband approaching. Howard is a smiler and a glad-hander, a deal maker. Let him talk to Mr. Nurture-the-Child's-Creativity. They probably work at adjoining law firms, probably play squash on the same courts at noon. Howard smiles at her and hands her a paper cup full of black coffee, and then he does indeed glad-hand the father across the table. Then, as Hannah takes a grateful scalding gulp of coffee and thinks regretfully about her own stiff inability to mingle, along comes Sophie, pushing up next to her mother at the table, butting another parent out of the way.

"Say excuse me," Hannah and Howard admonish in unison, but fondly. These two adults, who are so very different in their public selves, so very different even in their most private obsessions, have in common a bewildered appreciation of their daughter, of her determination, her resolute inability to notice obstacles, her oddly lovely turns of phrase. *She pushes us around like nobody's business,* Hannah has heard Howard boast to friends, as if his daughter were the sharpest litigator of them all.

"I am the only kid that is holding the gerbil," Sophie announces, thrusting the animal into her mother's plate of strawberries. Sophie, the child of two tall, brown-haired people, is a tiny blonde, a child with a triangular elflike face and masses of twisting blond tendrils.

Mrs. Peterson materializes, places a gentle hand on Sophie's shoulder. "I think it's a little too scary for the gerbil out here with all these people," she says, perfectly pleasantly. "Why don't you take your mommy and daddy over to the zoo corner and let them see how you put her back in her cage?"

Sophie's face freezes in an expression Hannah knows very well: thwarted, unable to believe that someone is trying to make her do something other than what she had planned, poised on the edge of screams, sobs, refusals. Hannah feels a sudden fierce triumph at seeing Mrs. Peterson's expert modulations meet with this response, but mostly she feels terrified that, amid all the other well-behaved parents and children, Sophie is going to make a scene.

"Does the gerbil live in a cage?" Hannah asks in wonder. "And do you know how to open it up all by yourself?"

"Not right now!" says Sophie. "I will show you, but I will show you later!"

Mrs. Peterson inclines her head at a professional angle. "Sophie, I am worried that the poor gerbil might be frightened. I know you are a very good helper with the gerbil, so I think you want to take good care of him — "

With the hand that is not clutching the squirming gerbil, Sophie takes the biggest strawberry off her mother's plate and pops it into her mouth. She chews. She ignores her teacher.

"Max," says Mrs. Peterson to a boy who has just brought more strawberries to the father across the table, "can you please help Sophie take good care of the gerbil? The gerbil *needs* to go back in his cage now."

Max's father, of course, videotapes Max as he makes his way around the table and reaches for the gerbil; he thus videotapes Sophie's lightning-fast evasive maneuver, her shriek of rage, and her diving attack, which leaves a set of teethmarks in Max's arm. Max begins to howl, and the gerbil drops softly and skillfully to the carpet. Hannah lurches to her feet, almost upsetting the small table, to go after Sophie, who has gone after the gerbil. Max's father, with his own loud "Watch out, there!" sets down his camera to inspect his son's wounds and therefore misses what would be the logical concluding shot: the gerbil, sensibly enough, making a run for it across the classroom floor.

Everyone behaves beautifully. Mrs. Peterson accepts the occasion as an opportunity to demonstrate her mastery of even difficult classroom moments. Max is comforted and Band-Aided, with everyone pleased to see that the skin is not broken. The gerbil, recaptured by Sophie in a dramatic body tackle, is tucked into his cage again by Sophie herself, who manages to convey that *now* it is the right time to put the gerbil away and who accepts her Time Out with a certain regal condescension. There is Howard, apologizing to Max's father, the two of them assuring each other that Kids Will Be Kids, with a certain amount of thinly veiled aggression in their voices, but maybe most of that is just their professional manners. And there are all the other parents, looking on with the smug, sympathetic concern of those whose perfect children have behaved perfectly. Still, Hannah reassures herself, these are all the parents of five-year-olds; surely they have all had to deal with public bad behavior at one time or another.

Leaving Howard to deal with Max's father, Hannah intercepts Mrs. Peterson, offers her own nervous apologies.

"Sophie loves animals," says Mrs. Peterson, "and I think she really wanted to share with you about the gerbil. One very important part of social development for kindergarteners is learning to respect one another, and there's always some extra tension when there are visitors." She smiles kindly and efficiently, and Hannah takes heart from this reasonable construction of Sophie's behavior: a generous-spirited animal lover, slowed in her age-appropriate development by the stress of the occasion. Together the two women look over at Sophie, who is sitting quietly in the Time Out corner, staring dreamily into space. Hannah's own stiff smile softens: *Oh, my willful beautiful mystery child!* Thank you so much, she tells Mrs. Peterson, with sincere and perhaps slightly overdone vehemence, thank you so much for making this room such a special place. I'm sorry Sophie got out of hand, but I know that overall she is having just a wonderful year. Thank you so much.

But then, as Hannah and Howard are leaving, Mrs. Peterson stops them at the door and asks if they would please schedule a meeting with her; she would like to talk to them about how Sophie is doing. When they have agreed and thanked her and escaped and are standing out in the school parking lot, Hannah and Howard look at each other, and though he tries for a wry shrug and she for a mock-helpless grimace, both of them know that this is no joke, and this is no good news.

⋆

They have, it seems to others, a somewhat odd and unexpected marriage. People are sometimes surprised to hear in those late-in-the-dinner-party, wine-tinged conversations that Hannah and Howard have been together since college, when she was a biology major and he was pre-law; even then their worlds did not overlap. Perhaps to those who know them now, they seem more like two people who might have met in their thirties, desperate to couple off. A personals ad, a hired matchmaking service, even a friend-of-a-friend connection: Hey, I know someone else who's very smart, very interested in settling down.

But it wasn't like that at all. Oh, they've had their summers apart and their doubts, but basically they are one of those peculiar and somewhat irritating couples who knew right from the beginning that this was it. What they have in common, what no one can necessarily see, looking at the straight-ahead trajectories of their careers, their relationship, their lives, is that they both believe the world is a strange and hostile place and the only hope for safety is in your home, your fortress, your secret sanctuary.

They take different approaches to this knowledge. Howard believes in getting out there and walking the walk and talking the talk and mixing it up with all comers. The law, for Howard, is a handy institutionalization of what he knows to be the truth of the world: me against all of you, winners and losers, attack or be attacked. Hannah, in contrast, believes in staking out a tiny territory, preferably a territory whose charms are invisible to most people, and staying low to the ground. As a fruit-fly geneticist, she is legendary for her compulsive care and caution; she will bring forward no results until they have been verified and reverified beyond all doubt. She will not whisper, not even dare to dream, what she has not protected and defended well in advance. She is careful, and she is talented, and when it comes to research, she has even been lucky. She can enjoy her success, but she will never relax and trust her luck. Never.

So now they live together with Sophie in one of those sunny big apartments that people live in right before they give up on the city and move to the suburbs for the sake of good public schools. But they will not move to the suburbs; they have promised each other that, and so they took Sophie through the private school dance and ended up at Dabney.

The night after their conference with Mrs. Peterson, Howard cannot sleep. He is pacing, fuming. Hannah at first does drift off to sleep, but she wakes up after an hour or so, disturbed by the crackling in the air, the tension in the room.

"Honey?" she says, shifting on her pillow. Then remembers: the classroom with Mrs. Peterson and the headmaster.

"That worthless lump of left-out Play-Doh," Howard says. The headmaster, that is. "That sanctimonious bitch." Mrs. Peterson, of course.

The headmaster's initial function at the meeting was to tell Howard and Hannah how proud Dabney was of Mrs. Peterson, the teaching awards she has won. Hannah nodded solemnly; Howard folded his arms and looked dubious.

Then Mrs. Peterson launched into her prepared speech: why Sophie is having emotional problems adjusting to kindergarten.

Soon, inevitably, Howard was fighting with her. And then with the headmaster, with both of them.

"Isn't that why you call it *choice* time?" Howard asked, with the exquisite, aggressive courtesy of a lawyer eager to trap a witness in the silken knot of her own words. "Because the child makes a *choice*?"

"Yes," Mrs. Peterson told him, "choice time is a chance for the children to exercise their own decision-making abilities in a safe and developmentally appropriate choice environment."

"So in that case," Howard said, "what's wrong with my daughter exercising her decision-making abilities?"

Patiently, as one who is well accustomed to helping distraught parents understand that their children have serious emotional problems, Mrs. Peterson explained yet again. "Sophie makes the same choice every day. She refuses to take advantage of any of the diverse learning opportunities that the classroom offers, and instead focuses in an unhealthy way on one small area of fantasy play."

"But if it's *choice* time," Howard roared, losing that exquisite courtesy, "then she's entitled to make any choice she damn well wants!"

The headmaster came to the rescue, explaining kindly and gently that this was not intended as criticism, it was just that Mrs. Peterson, with her award-winning skills, had picked up on some emotional adjustment difficulties that little Sophie seemed to be undergoing; the choice-time issue was emblematic of these stresses, which in turn might represent more serious home-based issues, which deserved attention before they got any worse.

It made Howard furious, and he's still furious now, in their bedroom. He's burning up with rage and with undelivered closing arguments. Hannah can see him mouthing words, forming phrases, silently testing out the crushing rebukes he never got to deliver — or, worse, the crushing rebukes he plans to deliver next time around. He does this before court appearances, and after them too, especially when things don't go well. Howard is clearly in combat mode. Villains are taking a swing at his most precious daughter, and they aren't even doing it as a dark and shameful secret. No, they have the nerve to act as if they're entitled to attack Sophie — but they clearly don't reckon with Howard's fierce loyalty and love, nor with his combative nature and his desire to win each and every encounter.

Hannah, lying in bed and watching him pace, loves him for it, yes she does. But it isn't clear at all to her that it will do Sophie any good to fight with her teacher and her teacher's boss. She would like to tell Howard that, but she is afraid he will see her as a traitor, betraying Sophie because of her own obedient good-girl instincts.

In the meeting, Hannah finally preempted Howard, who was obviously not at his best; she was grateful to him for galloping to Sophie's defense, but she knew it was the wrong strategy. You have to defer to their expertise; you have to listen to what they have to say.

"Tell us more about what's going on with Sophie," Hannah said, and Mrs. Peterson of course obliged.

The acting out. The rages. The yelling. The biting.

Howard took her up on the biting: how many times, under what provocation? The prosecuting attorney again. Hannah knew what he was thinking; at home, in day care, Sophie has been a screamer and a scrapper at times, but never a biter. In fact, Hannah felt a certain sense of triumph when Howard's cross-examination elicited from Mrs. Peterson the information that prior to the strawberry brunch, there had been only one biting incident involving Sophie, and on that occasion Sophie had bitten Emily only after Emily had bitten Sophie. Aha!

But this was the wrong tactic, and Hannah knew it. They needed to conciliate, to appear anxious to do the right thing, to be grateful for Mrs. Peterson's jargon-laced concern and the headmaster's orotund pronouncements. But all this was left to Hannah, and she struggled on alone, enduring Howard's looks of contempt and disbelief.

Sophie refused to learn to read. She just said she didn't want to, and she wouldn't, even though Mrs. Peterson had tested her on phoneme awareness and she was clearly ready. Hannah looked worried and said something about how much Sophie loved books. Howard demanded to know since when was learning to read *obligatory* for five-year-olds? Wasn't kindergarten supposed to be more about having fun? Why not leave her alone about it till she decides she wants to learn — she'll learn when she wants to, Howard assured them. There's nothing wrong with *her* brain, he added, looking straight at the headmaster.

"There are serious behavioral red flags here," said Mrs. Peterson steadily. "I am especially concerned about the choice-time problem and what it reflects about Sophie's emotional well-being and her adjustment issues." The headmaster nodded solemnly: the choice-time problem.

That night, after they made Sophie's favorite supper — macaroni with lemon-butter sauce — and hugged and kissed her into bed, Hannah and Howard polished off a six-pack of beer, and even with all the tension, even with Hannah angry at Howard about fighting with the headmaster and Howard probably angry at Hannah for not fighting harder herself, they managed to make themselves hysterical with laughter over the image of Sophie undertaking civil disobedience in the kindergarten rain forest.

The Great Choice-Time Scandal: Sophie spent each and every choice-time curled up among the green construction-paper lianas, the photographs of poison arrow frogs and venomous snakes. When the time came to dismantle the rain forest, to make way for the igloo for the Eskimo project, Sophie took up a position lying across the squares of green carpet remnants, hugging the trunk of a tree, and wept for hours.

Mrs. Peterson, placed in the position of the despoiler of the Amazon, gave way. She refused to play the role of the soulless multinational corporation, agreeing finally to Sophie's terms:

the rain forest would be left intact. So Sophie continued to choose rain forest at choice-time, alone of all the children, since the others had long ago lost interest. You have to admit, Hannah and Howard told each other, it's pretty funny.

So they drank the beer, a very unaccustomed weeknight indulgence for them both, and cleaned up the kitchen and made Sophie's lunch for the next day, and went up to bed themselves. But Howard could not sleep, and at two in the morning here they are turning on their light and hashing it out again.

"She's a fascist with a degree in early-childhood education," Howard said. "She's mad because Sophie is smarter than she is and has a stronger will. She wants to punish all of us."

"I think you're reading some of this in," Hannah says, sitting up in bed.

"I am not reading it in. This is thought control," Howard says. "This is a teacher who likes having her own way and comes up against a little girl who just won't take it from her." There is nothing in his voice but admiration and love.

"But honey, she does have to get along in school," Hannah says, and sees from his face that she has played the traitor. If you aren't with me, you're against me: that's Howard.

"What are you talking about?" Howard demands. "You think we should put a perfectly sane, intelligent child into therapy because her jargon-stuffed imbecile of a kindergarten teacher loses a few tugs-of-war with her?"

That is what they want, Mrs. Peterson and the headmaster. They even offered a list of approved therapists "who have worked well with Dabney before." Sophie is troubled and disturbed, ran Mrs. Peterson's summation; she will not learn to read, despite her high level of phoneme awareness; she demonstrates inappropriate emotional intensity in peer conflicts. She screams and she bites. ("Emily bit her first!" said Howard. "Max didn't," said Mrs. Peterson.) In addition, she is not open to the rich variety of learning and social opportunities offered by kindergarten: she refuses to have anything to do with marionettes, she would not wear pajamas on pajama day. "Pajama day?" Hannah asked, trying to keep her end up. "I didn't know you had a pajama day." Mrs. Peterson and the headmaster exchanged satisfied glances. Sophie had concealed pajama day from her parents. She needed therapy immediately.

"Come to bed," Hannah says. She'll be exhausted tomorrow. She opens her arms, and Howard comes and lies beside her; she switches off the light and fits her body up against his. He holds her, even kisses her neck. But anger is still the strongest emotion in the bed.

It's always a little bit of a lottery waking up Sophie, who, if left alone, would sleep well on toward noon. Hannah goes into her bedroom never knowing whether Sophie will come to life sweet and cuddly or as savage as a bear disturbed in hibernation. Then there are the mornings she seems to awaken with a well-established identity: "I'm Barbie!" she will announce, and the prudent thing to do is to say, "Barbie, good morning!" and wait patiently while she roots around on her shelves for the five Barbie dolls that need to be carried to breakfast.

This morning Sophie opens her arms to her mother, who kisses the top of her head. Sophie's curls are pulled into a ponytail while she sleeps; this prevents some of the worst tangles and therefore the most violent hair-brushing arguments. The weight of her daughter on her lap is at once so exotic and so familiar that Hannah is moved, especially on this particular morning, when she has to accompany Sophie to the therapist's office. All of Howard's hostile open resistance to Mrs. Peterson, all his private bluster about suing the school, has come to nothing.

There have been two more conferences and several notes sent home. If they want Sophie to stay at Dabney, this kindergarten, which she says she loves, where her best friends, Dennis and Cara, go, then Sophie needs therapy.

Howard, Hannah realizes, feels ashamed as well as angry. He will not even consider accompanying Sophie to the therapist. He acts, in fact, as if Hannah has betrayed them all by making the phone call, setting up the appointment. Yes, Howard admits, he did agree; yes, he did say it was time to go ahead and start therapy, but he wants nothing to do with the arrangements or the appointments. Hannah is angry at him for this, for acting as though she is somehow going over to the enemy, when all she is doing is what they have both agreed they have to do. And angry at him for resolutely refusing to entertain the possibility that something might really be going wrong with Sophie. Hannah is not used to being angry at Howard, not steadily and quietly for days on end like this.

"I think you should stop acting this way, I think you should come with me to the therapist, I think you should help me figure this out," she said to him when the appointment was set.

"I'll only make things worse," said Howard, doing the thing he never does, sitting over a pile of work at the dining room table, pretending to be too busy to talk to her. "You said it yourself — I irritate these people and then they take it out on Sophie. You're better off without me."

"That's *not* what I said. I just think we have to truckle to them a little bit — to their expertise. We can't go in and say the teacher is a fascist and the headmaster is a moron and neither of them knows anything about children, and then expect their chosen child psychologist to shrug and say, Sure, you're right, everyone in the whole world is wrong and you guys are right. Look, it won't kill us to go in and be polite, call him Doctor. Maybe he'll have something reasonable to say."

Howard looked up from his papers, a level and clearly hostile stare. "*You* go, *you* be polite, *you* call him Dr. Expert Professor. Whatever you think is necessary. I'm sure you're on the right track. You're much better off without me, because if the asshole starts in on Sophie and choice time and all that crap, I'll tell him exactly what I think."

Yes, it would be a bad thing for Howard to come and fight with the therapist, make this new enemy — and if he fights with the therapist, perhaps the therapist will get even by reporting back to the school that Sophie is severely troubled. Or that Sophie's father has a problem handling his anger, just like Sophie does. No, let Howard stay away. But Hannah is still steadily angry, and there are moments when, in the middle of her grown-up, busy, seriously scientific day, she finds herself staring into space and wondering, *Is everything ruined?*

Sophie, fully awake now, looks up into her mother's face. Dreamily, she smiles and says, "I know a way for you to love someone but be angry at them. You just tell them, 'I like you but I don't like what you did.' "

"Yes," Hannah says. "That's very true. I like that."

"I knew you would," Sophie says smugly. "That is why I saved it to tell you as your special treat."

Hannah wears the flowered dress and the blazer she sometimes wears on the first day of classes. She dresses Sophie in a flowered dress as well, and gives in to her with no argument when she announces that she is going to wear her party shoes.

Hannah's secret fear now is that the therapist will confirm the judgment of the teacher and the headmaster: this is a troubled child. Emotional problems, adjustment difficulties. Perhaps the therapist will look at Hannah, stiff in her flowered dress, and say, Well, what could you expect with such a mother? Hannah, who has kept herself so carefully defended all her life, realizes once again the most essential lesson of parenthood: the terrible vulnerability of the parent. If she put into words what she is feeling as she carefully pulls the car into traffic, what she would probably say is, *I don't want anyone or anything to change the way I think about my daughter.*

Back before that strawberry breakfast, it seems to Hannah, she lived in a happy fool's paradise, thinking the world saw Sophie as she and Howard did, charmed by a child's assertive originality. *If you had told us of a child who refused all the other kindergarten choices and spent all day in the rain forest, we would have been tickled by the individuality, the strength of character.* But that was not how her world saw Sophie, and now, most insidious of all, Hannah and Howard see her a little as that world does.

The therapist is a man about Hannah and Howard's age, with a bushy mustache and hair going in all directions and a paunch that strains against his shirt. He comes out to greet Sophie and Hannah in his nondescript waiting room — a couple of molded plastic chairs and some reasonably recent magazines. A door leads into his office, and through the doorway Hannah can see big plastic bins of blocks and toys.

He shakes hands with Hannah and explains to her cheerfully that he wants to spend this first hour with Sophie, just getting to know her.

"I have some toys in my office," he says, directly to Sophie. "It's right in there — the toys are out on the shelves. Why don't you go take a look and see if anything looks especially interesting to you."

"I am wearing my party shoes," Sophie informs him. Without a backward glance, she heads into the office.

Hannah stands there, looking at the therapist. Unfairly, she knows, she starts out by disliking him, by resenting that he even exists, that he is in her life. She distrusts him; she assumes that he is the enemy, in cahoots with the headmaster and Mrs. Peterson — but this is a dumb, counterproductive, Howard-like way to think. If Sophie has a problem, if she's having trouble in school, what's wrong with trying to help?

"Her teacher, Mrs. Peterson —" Hannah starts to say, then stops. What is she trying to say?

"I have a report from her school," says the therapist.

"Oh," Hannah says. Thinking, *In cahoots.*

"I haven't read it yet," says the therapist. "Just like I'm not going to talk to you first. We'll get to all that. But first I think I should get to know your daughter." He gestures to one of the chairs. "Make yourself comfortable." Then, as he goes into his office, as he reaches to close the door and shut Hannah out, she hears him say to Sophie, "Great shoes!"

She knows the way to the therapist's office by now, but Hannah drives more slowly than usual; she has become in every way more cautious, she thinks. There was a time when motherhood seemed likely to make her into someone she had never been, someone spontaneous and uninhibited and always ready for an unexpected giggle, but she knows now that she is the same old Hannah.

Howard has withdrawn completely. He is working harder than ever, out most evenings. When Hannah told him, "We have an appointment tomorrow at the therapist's — he wants to see the whole family," Howard looked briefly pained. "I probably won't be able to make it," he said, and she nodded.

But then she couldn't sleep. She lay awake silently telling him over and over why it was important for Sophie that they go, that the therapist see them as a united concerned family, and inevitably she segued into a harangue: How dare you leave this entirely to me, how dare you just take it for granted that I will do this and you don't have to, how dare you abandon me and abandon your daughter . . .

The truth is that although she can't help rather liking the

therapist, if only because Sophie seems to like going to see him, she still regards him as some kind of enemy spy. He will be sending reports to the school, and he will report that Howard didn't care enough to turn up. Well, everyone will agree, no wonder she's a troubled child.

Hannah lay awake and sent furious thoughts flying at Howard's sleeping body. Eventually she got herself up and read scientific journals on the couch till she finally fell asleep. Then in the morning, at the worst possible time, with Howard getting dressed and hurrying off to work, she brought it up. She was tired and she had a headache and she was in no mood to be tactful. She told him he should come, it was important. She told him it was some kind of typical male arrogance to assume that certain parts of being a parent were optional for him but compulsory for her. She told him he needed to do this, he needed to be part of the process of helping Sophie, they needed to do it together as a family, and Howard told her that now she was beginning to sound like a psychobabbling, jargon-jabbering imbecile herself. It went downhill from there, and he stomped out with his briefcase. Hannah, furious and full of her own quota of undelivered crushing responses, woke Sophie and took her to school, went to work and did not try calling Howard at work, not once all day, and of course left early because she had to take Sophie to the therapist. Melodramatically, sleepily, Hannah said to herself as she started her car in the genetics institute parking lot, *I have become someone who does not want to speak to her own husband, someone who is taking off time from work to attend to the needs of her troubled child. What's next?*

Is she a troubled child? Hannah still can't quite decide.

"Look!" Sophie yells from the back seat. "Look at my favorite store in the whole world going by outside my window!"

Her favorite store in the whole world is a five-and-dime. Well, what the hell. They are early, of course; Hannah always leaves extra time. She parks the car and spends seventeen dollars on whatever Sophie wants. A magenta plastic egg stuffed with chocolates. Two necklaces and six bangles. A white patent-leather purse with a mirror inside. Golden plastic clip-on earrings. And a small pot of Swedish ivy.

In front of them in line is an old lady not too much taller than Sophie, or so it seems from Hannah's height. The lady has wispy white braids pinned up around her head but drooping down out of their black bobby pins. She wears, like Hannah and Sophie, a flowered dress. But hers trails on the ground in back; the hem is coming down, drooping like her braids as she inches forward in tiny steps to the cashier. She is buying two bags of licorice and a nightlight, digging in a well-worn change purse. Her fingers, which are twisted, put the coins on the counter: a quarter, a nickel, a pair of pennies. The girl at the cash register waits patiently, and Sophie is absorbed in the contemplation of her earrings, but Hannah is impatient: just dump the money on the counter, for heaven's sake, and get it over with. A dime. Another penny. A nickel and a quarter.

Then suddenly the old woman's shaking fingers tear right through the thin leather of her change purse, tear the leather right off its metal rim. A cascade of coins falls to the floor, bouncing and ringing against the metal candy stand. Hannah stares, not immediately seeing what to do with the plant, the necklaces and bangles, the plastic egg in her hands. But Sophie thrusts the earrings into the hand of the old woman, who is staring at the devastation. "I will pick up your moneys all by myself," Sophie announces. "Watch!" And she is down on the floor scooping up coins. Hannah, putting down her purchases, bends to help her daughter, but Sophie waves her away, saying triumphantly, "I am the only one who knows where is the money that I didn't already get!"

Truly, Hannah thinks dizzily, there is something blessed

about this moment. Sophie puts the money into her new white patent-leather purse and presents it to the old lady. When the checkout girl has efficiently bagged the licorice and the night-light, she rings up their purchases, Sophie and Hannah's, without charging them for the purse.

"That's a good little girl you have there," she says earnestly to Hannah, handing over their bag. She is maybe eighteen, with her nameplate, *Tanya,* displayed on a full bosom, her fingernails the long red talons that Hannah has never had and Sophie would kill for.

Waiting outside the store as Hannah hurries them to the car, since they are now a little bit late, is the old lady, who puts one twisted hand on Sophie's head and looks intently into the little girl's eyes.

"There is a mirror inside the pocketbook so you can look at yourself," Sophie says from around one of the chocolates; she has already opened the egg and started in.

"I will, thank you very much," says the old woman, in an unexpectedly firm and rich voice.

They are not really late, five minutes at most, but the door to the inner sanctum is open, denoting that the therapist has already come out and looked for them. Feeling flustered, noting that Sophie's face is smeared with chocolate, Hannah leads her into the room, pulls a tissue from her pocket, and starts to wipe around Sophie's mouth — all before noticing that the therapist is not alone. Howard is sitting in one of the armchairs, rocking slightly on its uneven legs.

"Hi, Sophie," says the therapist. "You look like you've been eating something." Although she knows it's silly, Hannah cannot help wondering whether he will record this as some small tick against her as a mother: feeds her daughter candy. No wonder the child is out of control.

"Hi, Hannah," says Howard, almost shyly. She cannot remember ever hearing him sound like that.

"I have bracelets and a plant, but I put all the moneys in the purse and gave it to the lady and she said she would look at the mirror," Sophie announces to her father.

Hannah has gone over to stand beside her husband, who gets quickly to his feet and takes her hand. The therapist smiles at them both and gestures them down into the armchairs. Hannah would like to go on clutching Howard's hand, but she's too self-conscious.

"So, Sophie," says the therapist, "today your parents are going to spend some time with us."

Sophie smiles at him, bewitchingly, enchantingly, then wheels around and goes to a cabinet. With confidence she opens it and removes a family of flexible dolls. Carries them to another cabinet and removes a red bin filled with plastic jungle animals. Then sits down on the floor, her back to her parents and the therapist, and begins to move the dolls and the animals in a game, murmuring their conversation, too low to be heard by the adults.

"Is that what she's done the other times she's come here?" Hannah asks.

"Pretty much," the therapist says. "We went through all the toys I've got, and she settled on that combination of dolls and animals."

Howard swallows. Still not sounding at all like himself, he asks, "Can you help us understand what that means, doctor?"

Oh, Lord, he's rotten at this. He sounds like a man reading sentences out of a phrasebook in a language he does not speak. But he's trying.

"Well, I would say it means that your daughter is a child who knows what she wants," says the therapist, smiling. Sophie, perhaps hearing him, turns around briefly and favors the three adults with one of her charming, delicious flashes of teeth.

Howard waits until she turns back to the toys, then says softly, "So what happens now?"

The therapist considers the question, which has not been asked with any false deference or with any true hostility, which has in fact, Hannah realizes with love and relief, been asked only with desperate sincerity. "Well," says the therapist, "I would say that what happens now is we watch your daughter, who is without question a smart and determined little girl, and make sure her world is the place she needs it to be."

"She's fine, then," Hannah says definitively, to her husband and the therapist both.

Howard takes a deep breath; Hannah can actually see his shoulders rise and fall. She thinks of safety — not the feeling that she is in a safe place, but the feeling that perhaps it is possible sometimes to create safety, to bring it forth out of love and vigilance and even, perhaps, a little hostility and aggressiveness.

Sophie speaks: "Look what I can do!" Her parents and the therapist turn and look, and she holds out the magenta plastic egg. Dramatically, making extravagant gestures, she opens it into its two halves. "See, there is no candy inside anymore," she says, and Hannah nods, sees the other two nodding as well. Sophie puts her nose to one empty magenta egg half and takes a long happy breath. Lifts her face up, radiant with joy and surprise, and cries out, "Oh! As I sniff the chocolate air!"

And she puts her nose down to the egg again as her parents watch her from across the room.

The Province of the Bearded Fathers

On a bench in the sun at the side of a playground in Cambridge, Massachusetts. Willow, tall but heavyset, and her real name is Esther; she changed it way back in college and has felt silly about it almost ever since, but still secretly likes the sound. Janet, smaller and neater and possessing a Ph.D. Both of them eating ice cream sandwiches, licking grooves around the sides as the ice cream melts in the first real sun of summer, the first day actually uncomfortably hot.

The nearest piece of playground equipment is the mouth of a tall twisting slide, an orange plastic tube that spirals down from the top of a wooden climbing structure. Periodically the slide shivers in the sunlight, then extrudes a child into the sand, to pick itself up and hurry away.

Janet has a postdoc in the lab of someone so important that many people mistakenly assume he has already won a Nobel Prize; there is nothing that pleases him more than to hear this mistake made. Janet has just reported him to the university sexual harassment committee and wonders whether she has in one fell swoop ended her scientific career. She mentions this worry yet again to Willow, who is touchingly confident that someone as brilliant and talented as Janet will have no trouble at all finding a new lab to work in.

But then Janet begins to think about what this would involve, the politics of switching, of explaining why she needs to switch, and the logistics, pure and simple, of interrupting everything she is doing and moving and starting something new. She looks almost desperately around the playground for something else to talk about, points out to Willow that two small boys crouched in the shadow of the spiral slide are trying to build an elephant trap. They have dug a large square pit and are roofing it over with twigs and grasses, which keep falling down into the hole.

They have been friends since college, Willow and Janet. When the housing office first assigned them to be roommates, Janet was wary, wondering what they could possibly have been thought to have in common. Willow had so many friends; everyone on campus seemed to know her, and she knew, always, about every party. Fortunately, she and Janet did not actually have to share a bedroom; they had a big room and a small one which opened off it, and Willow slept in the little one, often with one boy or another. She was friendly and free, tall and thin and graceful (so the name made more sense), with straight hair down almost all her long back to her waist. She was a Romance languages major and a straight A student. Janet, also a straight A student (could the housing office possibly have foreseen this?), though in biochemistry, needed quiet to work and made friends slowly and rarely. Her life was serious; her work was serious. But outside the bright and busy kingdom of her mind, outside her own ambitions and her organized lists of what she had to do, she could see Willow dancing, skipping from boy to boy like a square-dance figure. Willow was her entertainment, her diversion.

More recently, Willow has been a problem; Janet tends to divide her life up into problems. The problem of Willow is that despite her magna cum laude, Phi Beta Kappa degree, she has never figured out what to do next. She taught French in a private high school for two years, but wasn't much good at it; the students liked her but learned very little. Then she did this and that and talked about going back to school for another degree, a Ph.D. in Spanish literature, or a master's in education, or maybe a law degree, but she never got beyond flipping through the catalogues. Instead of pursuing an advanced degree, she takes these silly adult education courses, flips through those catalogues too, and spends her money on evening seminars and weekend discussion groups. Right now she has one of the worst jobs she's had, brainless paper-sorting in a college admissions office. She doesn't even get to choose rooming combinations; that's done by computer nowadays.

Janet, though, has gone full speed ahead, and look where it has gotten her. She watches a thin, dark little girl with two long black braids emerge from the slide cautiously, tense and controlled – probably rode all the way down with her toes dug in as brakes. No sooner is she out of the way than two older boys shoot out into the sand, *whoosh whoosh,* and immediately continue the wrestling match that precipitated them into the slide.

Janet says, "I wish I hadn't done it, that's all. Why did I do it?"

Willow answers calmly, "You did it because he started calling you up at home in the middle of the night and saying weird things. You did it because you were scared to work in your own lab after hours and you were dragging all your nonscientific friends along to keep you company."

Janet is the kind of scientist who always works late nights and weekends. One night when Willow was there with her, the famous professor did in fact show up. He slipped into the lab almost silently; then, realizing he was not alone with Janet, he invented some lame excuse about a slide he needed to pick up. It was a creepy encounter, and Janet and Willow left immediately after he did, went to Harvard Square, and got drunk.

The little girl with the long braids comes out of the slide again, this time head first and at top speed; she has the same concentrated look on her face.

"It's like the spout of a machine that manufactures children," Janet says. "No fuss, no bother, no pregnancy — push a button and out they come."

Willow, who has a vague feeling that she might be pregnant, jumps up from the bench and heads for the water fountain.

"I'm sick of this, I'm sick of worrying about it," Janet calls after her. "Let's talk about your moral dilemma instead." In many ways, Willow is still her entertainment.

Willow's dilemma is that she's sleeping with a married man, with her landlord, who comes and knocks on her door while his wife is out working. Janet disapproves, though she is titillated. Willow argues that she is doing her landlord's wife a sort of favor; if he's going to stray — and he definitely is — isn't his wife lucky that he's sleeping with a woman who has no interest in breaking up the marriage, with a woman who only wants him for sex and wouldn't marry him on a bet? He isn't really a very nice person, Willow always says. Now she says it again, as if it worries her.

"I know," Janet says. "Not a very nice person. Just hung like a horse." This is Willow's stock phrase to explain what's in it for her, why she continues this sordid arrangement. The joke between Willow and Janet is to refer to this man as the Italian Stallion and to pretend that he is a terrifically sexy ethnic, Marlon Brando as Stanley Kowalski, the super coming up all sweaty from the basement to bang the lady on the second floor. This is a joke because his name is actually Brad Winterset, and he is a washed-out WASP from Nebraska who sits home all day supposedly finishing his master's thesis on the economic after-effects of the Korean War while his wife is out earning money doing family therapy. The two of them live on the first floor of an old Cambridge triple-decker, and Willow rents the second; up on the third is a shifting household of law students.

Willow has been quite content to make the affair into a tabloid headline: He Came to Fix the Sink and We Did It in the Bathtub. But what if she's pregnant? What then? Janet is someone who believes that carelessness with birth control is pathological, criminally stupid, maybe borderline crazy. Willow has already had two abortions. In fact, both times she brought home a pregnancy-test kit, the test was positive; therefore she is unwilling to buy a kit and test herself. *If I test myself, I will be pregnant,* she believes, *while as long as I don't test myself, it's possible that I'm not.* Makes perfect sense. No wonder she won't discuss it with her friend the scientist, who might expect action and decisions and plans. Would Willow have a third abortion? Or would she go ahead and have the baby? And would that suddenly make sense of her life: Single Mom Struggles Bravely?

The girl with the long braids is now attempting to crawl up the twisting slide, entering from the bottom, but she keeps sliding back down. The boys have abandoned the elephant trap, and a very small child wearing only a diaper is digging in the sand right there. Willow imagines the baby falling suddenly through a crust of sand into a pit. But of course there is no pit, only a shallow depression in the sand, which the baby is now happily erasing with her bright green shovel. Willow closes her eyes, leans back, letting the sun warm her face, thinking that Brad is not really an Italian Stallion, and he is also really not a very nice person.

A week later, on the same bench, Willow is beginning to feel sure she is pregnant. She is still shy about mentioning this to Janet, but she cannot get it out of her mind. *I'll give it two more days,* she thinks, *and then I'll buy the damn kit and do the damn test.* Of course, a playground full of children doesn't help much. It's another gorgeous day and the playground is hopping, and Janet is analyzing yet again what happened when the committee called her in and told her they would be following up her accusation with the greatest vigor, and then the next thing anyone knew, her professor had been temporarily suspended. This was reported with lascivious thoroughness on the front page of the campus paper and picked up by a wire service; Janet's name was not mentioned. The next day, two other women came forward with similar stories about the same scientist; one had been his secretary and one his graduate student, and both had left their positions, they said, because of his persistent sexual advances.

"You're a hero," Willow tells her friend for the twentieth time. "You did what no one else was brave enough to do."

"I never meant to ruin his life. I never meant for this to happen."

"Janet, the man is a pathological dweeb – he's a big-shot scientist who gets his kicks by calling you up at three in the morning to say he's coming over, be waiting for him naked with the butter at room temperature. You thought what – that the committee would slap him on the wrist and then you'd have a good working relationship?"

"Shh!" Janet looks frantic, and guilty, glancing around the playground to make sure no one can hear. "You shouldn't ever tell anyone else that story about the butter, you know."

"Or wrapping up his dirty underpants in foil and leaving them in your lab refrigerator?"

"Willow, keep your voice down! Please!"

Softly and gently, Willow says, "He's crazy, he's a jerk, he might even be dangerous. You did the right thing." There is a pause as both of them stare straight ahead. Then Willow says, with comic effect, "Men!" She is thinking about being pregnant, wondering whether she should go ahead and have the baby of this not very nice perennial graduate student. Will it mean, among other things, that she will miss her chance for the mutually supportive and warmly loving relationship with the nurturing and secure-in-his-own-masculinity fellow who is otherwise waiting in her next adult education course? "Men," she says again.

"I'll never get married," Janet says.

An unbelievably adorable little girl, right on cue, comes toddling past in a very grimy sunsuit, dripping popsicle in hand, pale blond curls stained with raspberry, her cheeks chubby and dimpled.

"Hi!" Willow says. The little girl stops and stares at them, then gives a shriek of laughter, dumps the remains of her popsicle in Janet's lap, and runs off to climb up the wall of rubber tires leading to the top of the climbing structure.

"Shit," says Janet, who of course is wearing white pants. "I'll never get married."

"A couple of years down the road it'll be you and me and the bambini here in this very same playground," Willow says. "Station wagons parked nearby. The whole bit."

"Not in this playground," Janet tells her. "We'd stick out like sore thumbs."

"What do you mean?"

"Willow, don't you ever notice what you're seeing? There aren't any mothers in this playground."

Willow looks around. It's absolutely true. Cambridge fathers, as far as the eye can see. Beards and blue jeans, academic pallor and witty T-shirts. Fathers pushing the swings and fathers climbing the jungle gym and fathers supervising sand play.

"What does this mean?

"I don't know. You probably have to be married to understand. All I know is, we always come here on Sunday afternoons, and on Sunday afternoons this playground is the province of the bearded fathers."

"God," Willow says uncomfortably. "All these groovy men." Is this what's waiting for her in "Wine Tasting" or "Fun with a Kayak"?

"Not for us," Janet says, sounding a little more cheerful. "For you it's the Stallion; for me, the less said the better."

"We could go split a pizza," Willow says. They have split many pizzas in their time, and it is well understood between them that the anchovy half is for Janet, the pepperoni half for Willow, but the split is three-five, so that Willow eats one slice of anchovy. They divide the cost of the pizza evenly, but by time-honored custom Willow springs for both Diet Cokes.

The goddamn big-shot famous scientist professor kills himself. But then again, Willow isn't pregnant after all. So she's in a pretty good mood, singing a little song she's made up for Janet:

"Once they put pennies on your eyes,
You can't win the Nobel Prize."

"Stop it. Please stop it. You don't understand how bad I'm feeling."

They are trying to eat brunch in a chic little patisserie, with tables so close together that when Willow announces in a perfectly normal tone of voice that she's not pregnant, people at all four adjoining tables look up with interest. Janet is also interested, even distracted, just as Willow hoped.

"You didn't tell me you thought you were pregnant."

"I was ashamed of myself."

But when she says that, Janet gives way completely, bursting into tears over her eggs Benedict, and Willow has to pay and hustle them both out. It's a rotten day outside, humid and foggy, with a sense of impending rain, but they wander over to the playground anyway.

Only a couple of children are in the playground, only a couple of fathers. Willow leads the way to the swings, and the two of them sit for a while, swinging back and forth in an uninterested way. On the third swing, right next to Janet, two little girls are doing acrobatics, standing face to face, swinging as high as they can, changing places in flight, solemn and graceful as trapeze artists.

"Perhaps one day they too will sit here, grown women with problems," Willow whispers with mock solemnity.

One little girl sits down on the swing and pumps energetically while the other stands up, her feet firmly wedged between her friend's thighs and the chains, leaning out as the swing rushes forward.

"He needed help, and I betrayed him," Janet says, as if trying on the trauma for size.

"He needed a good kick in the pants and you were terrified of him," Willow comments.

"There's such a lot he might have done, and now he won't, he never will."

"Well, there's a lot I might have done too, and maybe I never will, but that doesn't mean I go around leaving pictures of my genitals in other people's lab notebooks," Willow says, calm and offhand. And suddenly, remembering those clinically exact black-and-white snapshots, Willow and Janet are both laughing, and Janet, for the first time since the suicide, is thinking clearly about what she will have to do next, about how she will find a new lab to work in.

They leave the swings and climb the tire wall. It's easier than it looks; the tires offer unexpectedly secure footing. And there they are at the top of the wooden climbing structure, looking down at the almost deserted playground. There is the bench they have sat on, over in the corner. A rather forlorn bearded father is sitting on that very same bench, trying to comfort a howling little boy. From their pinnacle, Janet and Willow cannot tell what all the fuss is about. Willow is thinking she could go down and smile at that father and help comfort the boy, but she won't. Sleazy and immoral she may be at times, but she does not pick up married men in playgrounds. She thinks of the hour she spent with her landlord yesterday, his wife out at some downtown therapists' conference, Willow of course desperately relieved to have gotten her period, and old Brad Winterset, as usual, without the faintest idea about anything at all, performing the function for which God evidently designed him. The memory embarrasses her but also warms her, pleases her, and she smiles at her friend Janet, who is staring intently at a postal service truck parked on the corner.

My own lab, Janet thinks. *Someday, me in charge, my name first on all the papers. And hell,* she thinks, *now that he's dead, I'll use him as a reference. People will be impressed that I worked with him.* Then she feels frightened — *What kind of a terrible person am I?* — and covers her face with her hands.

Willow puts an arm around her. *Someday,* Willow was just thinking, *a real job, a purpose in life.* But what she says is, "I bet the high school students come up here to smoke dope."

Janet lifts her head and smiles, imagining herself as she was in high school, all seriousness and self-discipline. "And talk about life."

The whole wooden structure shakes as a troop of little kids comes up the tires, erupting onto the platform. Willow and Janet pull apart and watch as two red-haired boys dive headfirst into the twisting slide while the others crowd to the side to empty pockets full of pebbles over the rail.

A girl maybe ten years old, very sleek and collected, wearing black stretch leggings and a very large MIT sweatshirt down to her knees, comes to stand beside Janet. "They're playing that this is a fort and we have to defend it," she says with mild contempt in her voice. "They're throwing down stones. And the enemy might use a battering ram." Then, with no transition at all, she suddenly screams out, "Surprise attack from the rear! Surprise attack from the rear!"

The two redheaded boys are coming up over the other side of the platform, having bypassed the tires and climbed the more challenging log wall. The children stampede over to stop them, and the girl in the MIT sweatshirt calls out, "Stomp on their fingers!" Then she confides to Willow in an undertone, "Actually, what they would really do is pour boiling lead on the invaders."

The two boys fight their way up onto the platform, and all the younger children look at them expectantly. The smaller of the two, a freckled scarecrow who wears purple hightops, announces, "Spitting tag! We're gonna play spitting tag, and I'm gonna be it!" Immediately he begins to froth at the mouth like a rabid dog, and all the children shriek and scatter, down the tires, down the log wall, down the slide. The frothing boy goes leaping down from tire to tire, and Willow and Janet are alone in possession of the high ground once more.

Janet leans over the parapet, watching the playground. "Look, the girls are still swinging." They are still on one swing, squatting now, face to face, leaning their bottoms out into thin air.

It's getting windy, and the wooden structure sways a little bit. Willow sings into the wind:

> "When you kill yourself, you lose your grants,
> And your frozen dirty underpants!"

The wind whips her words away. Janet stands, holding herself, wondering if she'll cry again, wondering if she'll smile. The professor was someone she admired, someone she once hoped would think well of her, would shape her career. His life is over, truly, literally. Her life is not, she knows, but still.

Willow finishes her song and takes a bow, and Janet says to her accusingly, "You know what I think about people who take chances with getting pregnant."

"You'll find another lab," Willow says.

Janet takes a deep breath. "I guess so."

"Don't worry," Willow tells her. "After you get your life straightened out, you can deal with mine."

"Thanks," Janet says. "Thanks. You just wait and see."

Willow hugs her quickly, warmly, then continues past her to the mouth of the twisting slide. Janet follows after her, into the orange spiral and down to the ground.

Love and Modern Medicine

NO, I DO NOT LOOK AT MY PATIENTS, alive and wriggling, and think about sudden infant death syndrome. I mean, I do not stop and weigh those words, there in the exam room, as I weigh the baby. You've probably considered the term yourself at times — well, of course you have, we all have, all of us who've had babies. We've all thought and thought about every possible inflection of those words as we've leaned over cribs and bassinets and held our own breathing to hear the baby's more clearly, or laid a gentle maternal hand on a sleeper-covered tummy to feel the rise and fall.

I wonder about the word *sudden.* Suddenly the baby isn't. The baby was breathing and then suddenly the baby is not breathing. How does it happen, what are the final moments or seconds? We can picture it, as parents; we do picture it, as you know, we can picture a silent short struggle, perhaps — or is it just a baby sleeping slower and slower and slower until the sleep is final? But there's nothing sudden about that. Wrong word, then. Sudden means abrupt and out of the blue. Sudden means was and then wasn't.

I have never liked my half-sister. I suppose right from the beginning, just as her mother was my father's formulation of the right answer in his life, the smoother, younger antidote to my own somewhat difficult mother, I have tended to formulate

Deirdre in my mind as the perfect daughter / perfect girl / perfect mother, God help me. The one who is lovely, the one who is easily loved. The idiot, in other words. The fine female and feminine fluffhead. I made many jokes to my husband about Deirdre and what she would be like as a mother, steaming and pureeing the organic vegetables, double-washing every garment before it touched her baby's skin, keeping the baby book psychotically up to date. All the things that, needless to say, I don't do.

These are the kind of jokes you feel bad about when your half-sister's infant has been found dead in her crib at the age of six months. When she never got old enough to eat those pureed organic vegetables. And that truncated baby book — don't even ask.

Deirdre and I have not been close, not ever. I grew up ten years older, largely in the house of my mother, who was more than ten years older than Deirdre's mother and somewhat difficult, as I somewhat politely put it, and who was quite caustic on the subject of my father's second round of fatherhood with all its attendant sentimental discoveries. Did I love hearing over and over my mother's sarcastic comments on my father's second round of fatherhood? Did I enjoy her accounts of how oblivious he was during my own childhood, as if this were some kind of news? You guess. Do I cherish and cling to some forlorn hope that he will wake up to me and look over and glow with pride? Doubtful, but not, I suppose, absolutely impossible. He did come to my medical school graduation, and he looked both proud and on his guard: not his world, not his language, not his people. Made a bunch of dumb references to the money he had spent to get me through and then sat, a little bewildered, through a much too technical talk on the future of gene monotherapy — which has, by the way, more or less failed to live up to its promise, as far as I can see. Wonders of modern medicine.

Deirdre is now in my house, secluded in a very poorly heated room on the third floor that my husband and I have always called the guest room, hoping it will someday grow into a guest room, more or less without our help. She slips down at odd hours to use the second-floor bathroom (my hope was actually that the house would sprout an extra bathroom on the third floor to accommodate the guest room; I could imagine the pretty embroidered guest towels on their rack, and the imported triple-milled soap), assiduously avoiding my two children, my husband, and me.

I work part-time. My husband is a radiologist, so he has a reasonable schedule, but his commute to work is almost an hour and he gets home late. The HMO where I have my pediatric practice is only about two miles from the house, and I try to get home most days about an hour before the school bus. It is in that hour that Deirdre comes and finds me, brings herself and her tragedy to my sisterly and medical attention. But though half a sister may be better than none, I am not much use at all as sisters go, I think, and of course I and my whole profession and its wonders are useless in this instance.

"Some people in the support group go on marking the birthdays — or what would have been the birthdays." Deirdre sits at my kitchen table and drinks mugs and mugs of herbal tea. When she came she brought a whole suitcase full of nutritional supplements and medicinal herbs, and the witchy scent of her tea lingers behind her in the kitchen when the school bus pulls up and she flees. Back up the stairs and into her tower. "There's this one family — the parents came to talk to us — their son would have been six, they said, they already had two more children, younger ones, I mean, children born since their son died — and they still celebrate his birthday. They said the other children will always know that's a special day. They have a cake, they write his name on it. So that's six birthday celebrations, all without the child there."

I am silent. I never know what to say. Is this good? Is this bad? Is this comforting? When would Sara's first birthday have been, exactly? Sometime this month, but when? Oh God, what if it's today and I didn't know?

"I think that's kind of extreme, myself," Deirdre goes on. "I mean, I don't think it's really fair to the other kids."

Immediately I want to say, *But if it gives the parents comfort and the kids cake, is there really any harm in it?* But I don't say anything; as I see it, only one of the two of us is entitled to an opinion on this subject, and it isn't me.

She stirs wild clover honey into her mug, and more, and more.

"Sara would have turned one last month on the twenty-second," Deirdre says. As always, I shiver just slightly when she says the name. I can't help it. She doesn't. "She died just after her six months birthday. Three days after. I think about her six months checkup — I had an appointment for her the day before, but I changed it because I wanted to go to this yoga class for postpartum mothers. Maybe if I had taken her, the doctor would have seen something."

We have had this conversation before. And before and before. But surely it is the least I can do, in my pediatric incarnation, to sing the lullaby of modern medicine, to speak my lines as often as Deirdre wants.

"The doctor wouldn't have seen anything. There's nothing to see. This is something that happens to healthy babies. Suddenly. Out of the blue. No one can predict it, no one can prevent it." Am I boasting? Am I defending? Am I apologizing? What I am doing, of course, is thinking of my own two, boy and girl, now safely school age. Thank you thank you thank you. Does Deirdre know that in addition to everything else, mothers and fathers look at her now and touch wood? I touch the underside of the kitchen table, not for the first time. Mrs. Science herself. The doctor herself.

"Maybe there *was* something to see. Maybe things would have been different." You have to picture her, stirring more and more honey into her mug. Deirdre with her blond hair pulled tightly back into a ponytail, which hangs straight down her straight dancer's back. With her arching eyebrows and her high cheekbones. She looks like her mother, and I look like mine. You would know, I suspect, which was child of first wife, which was child of second wife. Scrubbed face and ponytail, she looks like an advertisement for whatever brew is in her mug: live healthfully, drink boiled weeds and seeds, and hope to look like me.

"Deirdre. If you had taken her to the doctor, the doctor would not have seen anything. Furthermore, the doctor would have given her her six-month shots, and then you would have spent the rest of your life wondering whether maybe the shots had anything to do with anything. I mean, I'm telling you they wouldn't, but I know you had doubts about Sara's getting shots."

I know that I met you once during Sara's short life, at a lavish family gathering in honor of our mutual father's seventy-fifth birthday, and that you held your lovely baby in your arms and stared at me accusingly and harangued me about compulsory immunization and its evils, every pediatrician's favorite topic. Deirdre, I said, you have to understand I give shots all day. I don't think I'm hurting children, I think I'm helping them. I invoked the deaths and miseries of diseases past, whooping cough and measles. Polio in the Third World, neonatal tetanus. But isn't *natural* immunity much stronger than the artificial manufactured immunity you get from shots, she asked me triumphantly. I said irritably, But you have to have the disease to get the natural immunity – which diseases are you willing to wish on Sara?

She clutched her lovely baby closer. Sara squirmed in her arms, blew a bubble, reached for a dangling earring. I touched her silly little blond topknot, wisps of baby hair gathered with a ribbon. Deirdre smoothed down the pink smocked party dress. Lovely baby, I said, lightening my tone.

In any event, her husband the software engineer put his foot down, and Sara did get her shots. And no one would have wished anything bad on Sara. No one.

But speaking of Deirdre's husband the software engineer, of whom we generally do not speak, something is occurring to me. A calculation.

"You came to visit right after Sara's birthday," I say, realizing. She called up – hi, this is Deirdre – as if she called all the time, and then, as if we ever visited each other, asked, Could I come and stay for the weekend? I need to get away, I just need to think. She has been thinking up there for almost three weeks now, and I cannot help wondering what she does all day. I mean, it's not like I come home from work to find her painting watercolors in the living room or baking organic muffins. Deirdre is hiding on my third floor, I assume hiding a little from the software engineer. From all her dear old friends, perhaps, who touch wood at the sight of her and go home to marital conversations in which blessings are counted and heads are shaken. From her support group of bereaved parents, perhaps, and their understanding. Or from her previous group, her all-natural pregnancy and new mothers' group (oh God, her mothers' group, that stalwart band of postpartum exercisers, busy I imagine with their leg lifts, exchanging half-baked pseudomedical information found on the Internet). Hiding from everyone kind and everyone who knows what's best for Deirdre. From her therapist, needless to say. Do I have to tell you that I had no stomach muscles to begin with, and that now, after two pregnancies, do I have to tell you what my stomach is like, that distinct laxness, those stretch marks? At work this week, I did a computer search of the medical literature and confirmed what I vaguely remembered: a large number of couples break up after a sudden infant death. It is, you would say, not a good marital prognosis indicator.

I do not know the software engineer. I did not attend Deirdre's wedding because I was not invited; it took place at a resort on an island in the Caribbean and featured, I am told (actually, I have seen a photo), a certain amount of beachside ceremony and an exchange of vows on a flower-strewn platform beside a waterfall; only a small group of most intimate intimates was invited (read, flown out by my father). So I have met the guy, the software engineer, exactly once, at that family gathering, and I shook his hand and told him he had a lovely baby. Sara. He talked to my husband, the radiologist, at length about gadgets and computer medicine. He said, It must be a pretty interesting job, being a pediatrician. Lots of crazy parents? Yes, I said, goes with the territory.

I have not, or perhaps not yet, had a SIDS death in my practice. Touch wood: I bump my knuckles gently on the underside of the butcher block table yet again. I have had two children die in car accidents, one hit in a crosswalk as he ran for the disappearing school bus, one killed in the back seat of the family car when a semi rear-ended them at a tollbooth plaza. I have had one leukemia death, and there is a six-year-old with a brain tumor who I am afraid may not make it. I mean, I have been to a funeral or two.

I went to Sara's funeral. *Lovely baby, lovely baby,* I kept thinking. It's a four-hour drive from my house in Massachusetts to

Deirdre's in Vermont. I left my husband and my kids at home. It rained most of the way and I drove a little too fast, as I have a tendency to do when it's only me in the car. I showed up slightly wiped out by the drive, found the house I had never before visited, greeted my father, Deirdre's mother, made medical conversation. No one knows. So many theories. Respiratory. Central nervous system. Persistence of fetal hemoglobin. Nobody knows.

We all cried at that funeral. A young woman minister with short burnished hair spoke her opening lines — Oh Lord, receive unto your arms this child Sara, something like that; Pick her up and hold her close, she said, cradle her gently, she is yours — and I started to sob, and so did everyone else. Up at the front of the chapel, I could see my father's white head sink forward into his hands, his shoulders heaving.

"Afterward," says Deirdre, "afterward you know it's kind of like you have to do everything for the first time. The first time you cook a meal. The first time you go to the drugstore and buy toothpaste. The first time you go to a movie. You have to decide that now you're going to do each thing."

"Yes," I say. "I see."

"The first time you go have coffee with a friend." She gestures to my coffee cup. "The first time you go to the post office for stamps. The first time you get introduced to someone at the post office and you don't even mention Sara so that person will never know you even had a child." She looks me in the eye, intense and focused. "The first time you have sex with your husband."

I can hear, very faint in the distance, the school bus motor. Years of listening at this very kitchen table have trained me; I am like the schoolbook Indians we dutifully learned about in social studies, who could sense the buffalo moving miles away. Once, a year ago, the bus did not come and did not come, and it turned out there had been a minor accident, the driver had bumped a parked car, and all the children had to wait while the police came and the reports were filed. Anyway, that day, sitting at my kitchen table and then walking out to wait by the curb, straining my eyes and my ears in the appropriate direction, I seem to have exercised and improved my acoustic muscles. Eventually, of course, I called the school and they knew all about the accident and were thus able first to make me frantic by saying, There's been a little accident, and then to calm me down with the details, but ever since that day of waiting and waiting, I swear I can hear that first rumble before there's actually any sound at all.

So I am on my feet and opening the door and hugging first one and then the other — of course, I hug them so much more now that Deirdre is haunting my house and my thoughts, but they don't mind, they're good, cooperative kids. Easy kids. Lunchboxes and backpacks and photcopied notices and library books and sweatshirts take over the entryway and the kitchen, and I put out glasses of milk and oatmeal cookies on the table. Deirdre, of course, has dematerialized, leaving only wisps of herbal steam to flavor the air.

Don't get a false idea. These oatmeal cookies are store-bought, though of upscale quality. Mom, I have to wear a white shirt and dark pants on Friday, we're singing in the assembly. Mom, can you come? Mom, I have homework, we have to finish our dioramas. Do you think Dad would know how to make them light up? Maybe we could use Christmas tree lights?

I think we should stick with nonelectrical dioramas, I say judiciously. And no, you know I have patients scheduled Friday morning, I can't cancel them on such short notice. You'll have to put on your white shirt and your dark pants and sing the song for us — a private performance. Who wants another oatmeal cookie?

Here's what they want, though: to go to the crafts store and buy posterboard for the Greek myths project (fourth grade, the girl) and a big Styrofoam ball to make a model of Mars for the solar system project (second grade, the boy). I attempt to point out that Mars the planet is in fact named for one of the gods in the myths, hoping to convince them that school is not just random bits of information, but my daughter informs me haughtily that Mars is the *Roman* god of war, and she isn't supposed to have anything to do with the Romans.

They like the crafts store. We will come home with packets of dyed feathers and funny buttons and I will find them in crevices around the house for months to come, along with all the fluorescent green and orange oversized pipe cleaners and the tiny pink pompoms from earlier trips.

Don't ask me why I mount the stairs to knock and invite Deirdre. Don't ask me why she comes. We belt ourselves into the front seat; the children click themselves into the back. I swivel and check: both belts properly fastened. Deirdre is our household goddess of safety; in her presence, all I can think about is what can happen suddenly. The skid, the crash from behind at the toll booth. Meteors can fall out of the sky and crush you, mosquitoes can bite you and transmit encephalitis. A baby can be breathing and then not.

My children are preoccupied, as usual, with the territorial division of the back seat; they squabble amicably enough as we drive into town. Yeah, but if I get a big Styrofoam ball, I get to put it in the middle of the seat. Dope, it won't be *that* big, you're so dumb, you don't know anything. Well, it'll be bigger than your piece of posterboard, I know that much.

A baby is so small and uncomplicated. When they grow up, when they go out into the world, there start to be all these details. School projects and dental appointments, nasal inhalers for the little one with his seasonal allergies, baseball shirts with the right numbers on them, fake tattoos and favorite radio stations. There they are out in the world, and what if someday the school bus doesn't come home and doesn't come home? But all you can do is belt them in and take them out in the world; look at Deirdre, look at Sara. Don't think that staying home keeps anybody safe, that's all I can say.

"He said that after the birthday we should start trying again," Deirdre says quietly, under the noise of my children sniping at one another. "He said, Let's use that as a mark — she would have been one, she's been gone for six months, it's time to think about moving forward. Moving forward."

I am driving, need I say, with exquisite care, moving forward along our familiar curving road at a speed that sends the pickup truck stuck behind me illegally into the other lane, passing us with a whoosh and an angry honk. Oh, Deirdre, goddess of safety. Of the sudden. Forgive me my healthy children and their noise, bless them and smile on them. I will do what I can.

"You will someday," I say, holding the steering wheel tight, making my minute corrections to keep us on course. "Maybe you're not ready yet, but you will someday. It won't make this not have happened, and it will seem very scary, but I believe it will happen. You'll be okay."

When I pick up a baby, I am often struck by the dense well-packed life, by the hum of all those miniature engines. Deirdre, will she always pick up her baby thinking about the other? Well, of course she will, at least a little bit. I know that it was Deirdre who found Sara in her crib, went to wake her because she had slept through her usual morning feeding. We have had the if-I-had-only-gone-in-earlier-would-it-have-made-a-difference-no-Deirdre-it-wouldn't-she-was-already-gone conversation even more times than we have had the six-month-checkup conversation.

When Deirdre found her, she was already cold. I cannot think about this, me with all my training, me with my children grown well into school-age safety.

Don't get me wrong; I have handled dead babies, dead children. I have even now and then watched them die. But the sudden part, the bending over the bed and reaching down and expecting the warmth and the softness and the clinging mouth. The hand that touches the body, the panicked realization that some soft and regular sound is missing, is silenced. I cannot walk my mind through it. Love and modern medicine, both useless.

We pull legally and cautiously into a space in front of the crafts store. Deirdre and I follow the children, who have launched themselves immediately on their searches. The aisle is lined with plaster objects to be taken home and painted: vases and pedestals, seated animals and angels. The next aisle holds metallic paints of every description, gold and silver and copper and every other color, glimmering greens and automotive reds. Deirdre touches a seated plaster cherub, a hideous smiling puppy, a jar of gleaming purple lacquer.

Finally we are in the Styrofoam aisle. My son has selected, naturally, the biggest possible ball, the size of a large pumpkin. We'll need red paint, Mom. Mars is the red planet, did you know that? He thrusts the ball into my hands and goes off in search of color.

Deirdre takes the ball from me. She is tall and queenly and lovely in the Styrofoam aisle, lovely especially when she smiles. She smiles. "It doesn't weigh anything," she says.

But it will be a planet when we're done with it.